FATED
BLADES

OTHER TITLES BY ILONA ANDREWS

The Kinsmen Universe

Silent Blade
Silver Shark
A Mere Formality

Kate Daniels World

Blood Heir

Kate Daniels Series

Magic Bites
Magic Bleeds
Magic Burns
Magic Strikes
Magic Mourns

Magic Dreams
Magic Slays
Gunmetal Magic
Magic Gifts
Magic Rises
Magic Breaks
Magic Steals
Magic Shifts
Magic Stars
Magic Binds
Magic Triumphs

Hidden Legacy Series

Burn for Me
White Hot
Wildfire
Diamond Fire
Sapphire Flames
Emerald Blaze

Innkeeper Chronicles Series

Clean Sweep
Sweep in Peace
One Fell Sweep
Sweep of the Blade
Sweep with Me

The Edge Series

On the Edge
Bayou Moon
Fate's Edge
Steel's Edge

The Iron Covenant

Iron and Magic

FATED BLADES

ILONA ANDREWS

Montlake

Text copyright © 2021 by Ilona Andrews, Inc.
All rights reserved.

Published by Montlake, Seattle

www.apub.com

Amazon, the Amazon logo, and Montlake are trademarks of Amazon.com, Inc., or its affiliates.

ISBN-13: 9781662500435
ISBN-10: 1662500432

Cover design by Faceout Studio, Lindy Martin

Cover illustration by Luisa J. Preißler

Printed in the United States of America

Of all the families in New Delphi, beware the secare the most, my son.

We are kinsmen. Our ancestors have enhanced our bloodlines to help humanity spread across the stars. All of us have trained for the art of individual combat. We are faster and stronger than an average human. We are duelists, but the secare were bred to slaughter. They excel at mass murder. That is the sole reason they came to be. It is our saving grace that the two secare families hate each other more than they detest the rest of us.

Avoid conflict with the secare at all costs. Should an opportunity to compete with them present itself, let it pass you by. Do not become their enemy, and better yet, do not become their friend, for there can be no peace between the Baenas and the Adlers. Sooner or later, they will clash again, as their foreparents have done generations ago, and if you ally with one of the two, you will find yourself facing the bloodred glow of the seco blade.

Should you ever encounter two secare who move as one, abandon your pride and run, my son. For your life is more precious to me than any treasure in this galaxy.

Henri Davenport Letters to Haider Davenport
Planet Rada, Dahlia Province,
City of New Delphi

CHAPTER 1

Rituals brought order to the chaos of life. Order was something Matias Baena deeply cherished, and so every Monday, at precisely 7:00 a.m., he entered his office on the top floor of the twisted blade that was Baena Tower and spent the next three hours sorting through the issues that had accumulated during the weekend. He read everything, organized it in order of priority, and formulated an action plan. At precisely 10:00 a.m., the small team of his top people entered his office to offer their insights and receive their marching orders.

Monday morning was sacred. The office door remained shut, the vid display refused incoming calls, and visitors were told to wait, no matter who they were. Nothing short of an attack on the building would warrant an interruption, so when Solei slipped through the door, Matias raised his head from R & D's progress report and braced himself.

The chief security officer looked unperturbed. Of average height, with the lean, powerful build of a combat athlete, sandy skin, and pale-blond hair, Solei had been a civilian for six years, but his composure had been tempered in hundreds of space battles. He would report a small leak and a planetary invasion with the same controlled calm.

"Yes?" Matias asked.

"Ramona Adler is here."

He must have misheard. "Define *here*."

"She's waiting in conference room 1A."

"Waiting for what?"

"She would like to speak with you. Privately."

If Solei had announced that his dead father had risen from the grave and was waiting outside the door, Matias would have been less surprised.

Of all the kinsmen families Matias disliked in the city of New Delphi, and he detested most of them, the Adlers were the only ones he hated. It wasn't a personal hate. It was generational. He had inherited it the way he had inherited his father's black hair and his mother's hazel eyes. Both the Baenas and the Adlers had arrived on the planet at about the same time, settling in the same province and inevitably doing business in the same city, both possessed about the same amount of territory and resources, and more importantly, both were secare.

The two families had clashed repeatedly over their first 150 years on Rada. The last outburst of violence had taken place when his grandfather was young and ended without any formal ceasefire. The two sides had nearly wiped each other out and simply couldn't continue to fight. Since then, the Adlers and the Baenas had settled into icy hostility, always watching each other, always ready for the feud to flare into raging violence. The animosity was mutual and deep. And now Ramona Adler waited in his conference room.

What was so important? Their policy of avoidance was working well so far. When forced to be in some proximity in public, he and Ramona painstakingly pretended the other didn't exist, and the kinsmen society, which had a long memory, enthusiastically supported their strategy of evading a bloodbath. They were never seated near each other. They were never formally introduced to each other. They never had a conversation.

Ramona could have called. Instead, she marched into his den and demanded to see him. She knew he could react with violence.

Normally, he might have called this reckless, except Ramona Adler was anything but. He had studied her since he was in his teens because she was a potential enemy, and he knew her as well as he did his own family. Ramona was like one of the smoke-furred foxes that inhabited the deep woods in the north, careful, calculating, and subtle. She struck only when she had complete confidence in her success, and she was lethal.

He had to know why she was here, and there was only one way to find out.

Matias rose and strode out the door. Solei turned with crisp precision left over from his military days and followed him, a vigilant, silent shadow.

The conference room lay at the other end of the tower, separated from Matias's office by a hundred meters of hallway. The Baena building borrowed its shape from the unfurling seco blade that gave the secare their name. It began as a wave, a low curve of plastisteel wrapped in panes of dark solar glass, dipped, then suddenly surged upward to the height of seventy meters, expanding into a hard vertical plane. A not-so-subtle warning.

The glass brightened as it climbed, and here, at the very top of the building, the panels were a deep, vivid red. The tinted light flooded the hallways through the translucent ceiling. Normally, he found it soothing, but today the air above the black floor seemed drenched in blood.

Most kinsmen didn't know where their unique abilities came from. Their beginnings had been lost to centuries of galactic expansion. The secare were different. All of them traced their origins to the Second Outer Rim War, when two budding interstellar empires clashed over a resource-rich cluster of planets. The brutal conflict lasted for sixty-two standard years, and the secare had been genetically engineered for that war.

While massive spaceships collided across the star systems, spitting energy and missile salvos, the secare fought in close quarters with seco weapons embedded in their bodies. A tool like no other, the seco technology allowed its owners to project short-range force fields from their arms that could become a shield or a blade in an instant. A seco shield could absorb an energy blast and stop a stream of projectiles. A seco blade could slice through solid metal like it was warm butter.

The secare had developed their own martial art, shifting between assault and defense in the blink of an eye. They were the silent dagger to the blunt hammer of the space armada, and the Sabetera Geniocracy used them again and again to bleed their opponents dry.

The war was long over, and the few remaining secare had scattered through the galaxy. Once comrades in arms, now the secare avoided each other at all costs. It was one of the universe's great ironies that after running halfway across the galaxy to get away from each other, both the Baenas and the Adlers ended up in the same sector, on the same planet, and in the same province.

The Baena family was guarded by state-of-the-art security. Matias oversaw it personally, and he hired only the best. All his guards were seasoned veterans with combat implants and skills honed by training and battle. They were well armed and ready. And if he felt like it, he could kill everyone in the building in minutes. It would be a massacre. They would know that he was coming, and all their experience and weapons would do them no good.

If he could do it, so could Ramona. The secare were killing machines, and the six generations separating them from a long-forgotten war had done nothing to change that. If she snapped, he would be the only barrier between her and the slaughter of his people.

Why was she here?

"How did she get into the building?"

"She walked in," the CSO said. "Our security intercepted her, and she told them that she'd come to see you. They called me. It seemed prudent to control the situation by escorting her to a secure room, away from civilian personnel."

They both knew that Solei's control of the situation was an illusion. Ramona could leave that room any moment she wished. And Solei's people would sacrifice their lives to keep the other employees safe until he got there.

"Good call."

"Thank you."

They reached an ornate double door. It whispered open at their approach, and Matias entered a large crescent-shaped room. The wall opposite the entrance was curved red glass, presenting a distant panorama of New Delphi. Between him and the glass wall stood a large oval table, carved from a single massive chunk of Gibirus opal. The mineral inclusions within the stone reacted to light, fluorescing with shifting ripples of color—fiery red, glittering gold, and splashes of intense emerald—setting the table aglow from within. Ramona sat at the table, her back to the window, her face lit up by gem fire.

He had never observed her from this close.

Twenty-eight years old, average height, athletic build of a practicing martial artist, long brown hair, features most people would find attractive. All things he already knew from images, recordings, and occasional cursory glances during the handful of times they had found themselves in relative proximity at formal events. None of it had prepared him for her impact at this range.

The difference between her images and reality was shocking. Like seeing a recording of a brontotiger taken with care under perfect lighting versus turning around in the middle of a hike and finding a pair of golden eyes staring at you from the brush.

Her hair was a warm chocolate brown. She hadn't bothered to put it up, and it spilled over her white jacket down to the curve of her breasts. The red light from the windows played on the dark strands, coaxing auburn highlights from the mass of loose waves. Her face was a soft oval, with a small but full mouth and high cheekbones. Her nose had a tiny bump on the bridge.

A narrow white scar, about two centimeters long, traced the curve of her bottom lip, stretching just under it to the corner of her mouth. She had killed the kinsman who gave it to her. She'd cut him in half, from right shoulder to his lowest left rib, with a single strike. The recording of it made the rounds. No other family dared to attack the Adlers after that.

Her eyes, a bright, startling blue, looked at him without fear or apprehension. She sat with a calm assurance, her body supple and elegant in a simple white pantsuit. She knew she was strong and fast, and that confidence showed in the tilt of her head, in the line of her shoulders, in the way she held herself. She could jump onto the table in a fraction of a second and dash toward him, her forearms releasing the seco and shaping them into lethal blades. A part of him would've welcomed it. He had never fought another secare outside of the family training hall.

He wanted to keep looking at her.

He wondered how fast she was.

He wondered if he was faster.

Ramona raised her eyebrows slightly.

He had to say something or do something. He couldn't just stand there, gawking like an idiot.

Matias took the closest chair and waved his hand. The ten guards positioned along the wall lowered their weapons and walked out. Solei lingered. Ramona looked at the CSO with her disturbing eyes and then looked back at Matias. He felt a sudden urge to do something dramatic and impressive.

He needed to get ahold of himself. She was in his territory, in the building he owned. He already had her undivided attention.

Matias dismissed Solei with a nod. The CSO withdrew, giving Ramona one last warning look. The door shut behind him.

Matias fixed her with his stare. "To what do I owe the horror?"

"I came to ask two questions."

Her voice suited her, a rich, smooth contralto.

"Very well. I'm all ears."

"Do you know where your wife is?"

His brain skipped a beat, then kicked into high gear. It wasn't a threat. If the Adlers had kidnapped Cassida, the ransom demand would have been delivered via a message. There was no reason for Ramona to put herself in danger.

He accessed his implant. A translucent interface overlaid the vision in his left eye. He selected Cassida's name from the contact list and waited.

A second passed.

Another.

A third.

She should have answered. Her implant would have recognized his call and linked with his even if she was unconscious. Either her implant was removed, which meant Cassida was dead, or she had deliberately blocked his calls.

"No answer?" Ramona asked. Her tone was perfectly neutral, but somehow, he felt mocked.

"Fine. I'll play. Where is my wife?"

"I wish I knew." She slowly reached into her jacket, withdrew a small tablet, and placed it on the table. "But I think he does."

On the screen, Cassida ran across a small, paved lot, her bright golden dress flaring around her, her auburn hair flying, as she sped toward a blond man waiting by a late-model aerial. He opened his arms, and Cassida jumped onto him, wrapping her legs around his hips.

A wave of ice splashed Matias and evaporated into intense, furious heat. His left hand clenched into a fist under the table. His wife was cheating on him.

Their marriage wasn't perfect. Strictly speaking, it wasn't loving or passionate, but it was perfectly amiable. He had remained faithful to her since their wedding almost three years ago. It never crossed his mind that she wouldn't do the same.

Ramona was looking at the screen with an odd expression. Not pain, but rather resignation. "The unbridled joy seems unfair."

"What is the point of showing me this?"

"That's the wrong question. The right question is, Who is the man she's climbing?"

She zoomed the recording with a flick of her fingers, and he saw the man's face—golden tan, square jaw, glowing with health and that particular polish that came with wealth and too much grooming. Recognition punched him.

"Your wife is having an affair with my husband," Ramona said.

For a moment they shared a silence as he came to grips with Cassida licking the inside of Gabriel Adler's mouth.

Ramona spoke first. "That brings me to my second question. Have you experienced any security or data breaches in the last few weeks? Go ahead. Check. I will wait."

Matias surged off the chair and out the door. In the hallway, the guards saw his face and flattened themselves against the walls.

"She does not leave," he growled. "Solei, with me."

~

Thirty minutes later Matias marched back into the conference room, and this time he didn't bother to sit down.

Ramona offered him a bitter smile. "She took everything?"

He didn't answer. The humiliation was too deep, and his rage burned too hot.

For the last two weeks Cassida had used his credentials to log into their files from his home office. He had no idea how she'd obtained his password, but with the proposal deadline approaching, he had worked from home with increasing frequency, logging in after hours. Her activity hadn't raised any alarms. She'd copied the entirety of their seco research.

"Gabriel has done the same," Ramona said.

They were sharing a rapidly sinking boat.

Until three years ago the technology of the seco had been lost. The seco weapon was a marvel of bioengineering. In its initial form, it was a hair-thin glowing strand visible only under strong magnification. When examined through nanoscale imaging, the strand turned into an ethereal narrow ribbon knitted from a million nanobots. It floated in the buffer solution, undulating and shifting, waiting for its host. When the time came, it and its twin would be implanted into the forearms of a newborn from a secare bloodline.

If the baby didn't inherit the secare ability, the ribbon would harmlessly dissolve within a year.

If the baby was born secare, the glittering constellation of nanobots would anchor itself and grow for another twenty-five months, forming a subcutaneous channel along the front of the arm until eventually the skin would split, allowing a microscopically narrow ridge to rise to the surface. It was invisible to the naked eye and too small to be felt by touch, but he knew exactly where it was. If he held his arms straight out, palms down, he could almost see the ridges running from his elbows to his wrists. When he wanted a blade, the seco burst forward over his wrist. When he wanted a shield, it fanned out from the entirety of his forearm, projecting into a shape he required.

The secare started training their children as soon as they could walk. They used the seco, they killed with it, and they replicated it, but nobody fully understood how the strands worked or why some children from secare bloodlines could use them and others couldn't. The secare were never trusted with that knowledge by their creators.

Then, three years ago, a salvager had stumbled onto a forgotten Sabetera Geniocracy lab in a random asteroid field. He brought the data banks he found there to Rada, sold them to the Baenas, to the Adlers, and to a third kinsmen family, the Davenports, letting everyone think that the sale was exclusive, and got the hell off planet as fast as his ship's drive would carry him.

The recovered intel opened the door to the creation of seco force fields by industrial means. Oh, it would require significant power and complex machinery to accomplish this, but it would blow conventional shields installed on modern warships out of the proverbial water. Bringing seco generators into mass production promised enormous benefits.

It also required a huge infusion of cash. Between the cost of rare metals, the custom nano cultures, and the cutting-edge tech required to retool the field to work without the biological component, developing the prototype would drain the Baenas' savings to nearly nothing. They could lose everything they had built over the last seven generations, but if they succeeded, the family would be stabilized and well funded for centuries to come.

The secare were born risk-takers.

Nine months into the project, Matias realized that they were in a three-way race. The space sector offered only one industrial partner capable of mass-producing the seco generators. Whoever successfully pitched their idea first would reap all the spoils. All three families abandoned their other projects and shifted all their resources toward building a successful prototype.

Now Cassida was on the run, and a copy of the Baenas' entire research was on the run with her. And so was Gabriel Adler with all his family's work.

Matias unclenched his teeth. "What are you offering?"

Ramona narrowed her eyes. "I know my husband. This wasn't his idea."

"He's off with my wife and your research. Now isn't the time for sentimentality."

Ramona shook her head. "Don't get me wrong. I don't mean to imply that he is an innocent pawn and your wife led him astray. But Gabriel lacks any sort of ambition. He has very little self-discipline, zero interest in business, and no knowledge of kinsmen politics. As long as he is fed, given an ample allowance, and allowed freedom to indulge himself, he's perfectly content. He is too lazy to start this adventure on his own. I'm in awe of your wife. She has managed to motivate him in a way I never could, and the universe knows I've tried."

"Cassida is very good at motivating." She had mounted a relentless assault on his peace of mind since the moment they'd married. He thought they had reached an understanding. Apparently, Cassida simply shifted focus to a more receptive target.

"Time is a factor," Ramona said.

He understood what was left unsaid. The stolen research would be sold. That sale would bankrupt their families.

"Cassida wouldn't have left without lining up a buyer," he said. "She isn't always prudent, but she is shrewd. She knows that the moment I discovered the theft, I'd go after her with everything I've got."

Ramona nodded. "I thought as much."

They had to move now. They had to recover the research, and they had to do it quietly. On Rada, a kinsmen family's standing was vital. It could mean the difference between being targeted in a feud and being invited to a negotiation table. Deals were offered and agreed upon based on the respect afforded to one's family name.

The secare enjoyed an aura of menace. Both families had been attacked, and both he and Ramona had delivered a gory object lesson that the city wouldn't soon forget. Most of their rivals considered a direct conflict with them out of the question. If it became known that not only had they suffered a catastrophic data breach, but their spouses had done it and then run away together right under their noses, their reputation would be in tatters. They would be disgraced. Even if they recovered the tech, they could no longer negotiate from a position of strength.

If speed was first, secrecy had to come second. Involving their families would only hinder them. He trusted his relatives with his life but not with his secrets.

"Who else knows?" he asked.

"The chief of cybersecurity and Karion," she said.

Her older brother. He wouldn't talk.

"I know my husband, but I don't know your wife." Ramona met his gaze.

"An alliance?" He raised his eyebrows, pretending to be surprised.

"A temporary one. Not between our families or our companies. Only you and me. We go quietly, we find them, we recover our assets before they destroy us, and then we never speak of it again."

Ten minutes ago, as the cybernetic security department fell on its figurative sword in front of him, his brain had already cycled through the possibilities and arrived at the only possible course of action. He'd been going to propose the same thing, and if she'd balked, he had a list of arguments ready to convince her. She'd saved him the trouble. If only his enemies were always so obliging.

Ramona was waiting for his answer.

He let her wait for another breath and nodded. "Agreed."

～

Matias Baena was something else.

Ramona leaned back in her seat and listened to him issue a flurry of orders to his CSO and Ladmina, his VP. He rattled off a quick, succinct rundown on immediate corporate tasks referred to in a manner that told her next to nothing about their true meaning and moved on to a catalog of things he required.

A fast, untraceable aerial with a survival kit.

A threat assessment on the Davenports, the third family with access to seco tech.

An internal lockdown on all information associated with the data breach.

A gag order and an expungement of her visit this morning, erasing all traces of her presence in the building from their surveillance.

An immediate implementation of a monitoring protocol tracking Cassida by implant and banking activity and both Cassida and Gabriel through a face recognition algorithm. If his wife spent any money, appeared in range of any cameras accessible by the public, or attempted to leave the planet, Matias would know about it.

He must've constructed a thorough list in his head, and now he methodically went through it, knocking items off one by one without a pause. Nothing was left to chance. He'd dissected the situation into chunks and addressed every aspect.

Precision was the quality secare prized most.

He acted like a secare, and he looked like one too. Her family kept the archival footage of the original unit, and she had watched it so many times over the years she could likely draw them from memory—the lean, strong soldiers in identical charcoal black, hardened by battle, stripped of all softness, with eyes that warned you off. The space crews developed the spacer stare, a haunted, distant look. The secare stared at you like a pack of human predators.

With his powerful body in a black doublet and his chiseled, harsh face, Matias would've fit right in, but it was the stare that cinched it. The scalding-hot stare of a hunter.

She had always thought he was cold, a closed-in, distant man with a stern glower. Someone capable of rationalizing cruelty. Someone who didn't bend because he couldn't be bothered, who never lost his composure. Impenetrable, like a chunk of obsidian. Who knew there was fire under all that volcanic glass?

A stray thought flickered through her mind. *It must be so nice to have someone like him watching your back. Someone competent. Decisive. Someone who has his shit together. Too bad he is an enemy.*

Earlier that morning, Ramona had sat in her office alone and viewed the two recordings of Gabriel, the first showing him stealing their data and the second of him meeting Cassida. She remembered the exact moment her brain processed what she was seeing. She felt a blinding pain, and then she went numb.

There was no time to feel or to come to terms with anything. She had to save the family. The emergency was so dire it pushed all her emotions out, leaving room for nothing else.

She had to hunt Gabriel down. She had two brothers, her parents, two aunts, an uncle, and a handful of cousins, and yet she had no one to turn to. Karion might have joined her, but she needed him to hold on to the family while she was gone. Santiago, her younger brother, was barely twenty and lacked patience. He would fly off the handle, and that was the last thing she needed now. None of the other relatives were secare, except for her retired parents, and she would rather die than get them involved.

She was on her own. At the time she had simply accepted it, but now, as she listened to Matias, she felt a crushing realization—she was alone. Utterly, completely alone. She would never let it stagger her, but it hurt.

The CSO and VP departed, Solei giving her a cold, flat stare before he left the room. Matias tapped the corner of the desk, and the ethereal light screen materialized on the wall. An older woman appeared, sitting on a garden bench against the backdrop of heavy dahlia blooms, her skin a deep brown tinted with red, her silver hair braided into a thick plait wrapped in an elaborate gold mesh.

"Aunt Nadira," Matias said.

After Matias's father died, his mother sank into her grief, abandoning her post as the leader of the family. Nadira jumped into that pilot seat before the Baenas had a chance to drift off course and steered the family for another eight years, until Matias was ready to take over.

She looked so harmless now, just an older woman in a beautiful emerald sari, surrounded by dahlias blooming in every color. And if an intruder broke into that garden, they would die before they ever sensed her presence.

Nadira smiled. "And how is my favorite nephew?"

Matias leaned forward. "Incredibly concerned and saddened by your recent illness."

She raised her eyebrows. "Am I sick enough to require your immediate presence?"

"You are."

"And am I refusing all visitors except my precious nephew because he is the only one I will allow to view me in my sorry state?"

Matias nodded. "Exactly."

"The shit has hit the fan, I take it?"

He moved his fingers right to left. The sensor in the vid screen obeyed, tilting it toward her. Ramona met the older woman's gaze.

"Oh," Nadira Baena said. "*That* bad?"

He tilted the screen back and nodded.

"How long?"

"As long as it takes."

"Very well. I'll have Sylus inform the family." Nadira leaned toward the screen and fixed her nephew with a sharp stare. "Watch yourself. Come back alive."

"Always." He kissed his fingers and offered them to her.

The display vanished.

"I can't simply disappear," Matias said.

It was an issue she was intimately familiar with. "The problem with spearheading a family business is that most of the corporate officers are also your relatives, who view you as the ultimate arbiter of their disputes."

"Yes. And in my case, they make no distinction between an argument over the precise calibration of the Kelly-particle agitator or the choice of a faucet for a new heated bubble tub."

"Same."

They shared a look. They were still enemies, but even enemies were allowed latitude when it came to complaining about family.

He rose. "The aerial is ready. Do you need us to stop anywhere?"

She had taken care of her affairs this morning. If her plan to convince him to cooperate had failed, she would have gone at it alone. "Everything I need is in my vehicle. I'll give your people the code. They can bring it up."

"Perfect." He approached the door and waited as it slid open. She walked through the doorway, presenting him with an unobstructed shot at her back. If he struck, it would be now.

Matias turned left. "This way."

They headed down the hallway to the same private elevator she had taken this morning, except this time there wouldn't be six armed guards in it. Just her and Matias Baena.

She had lost her damn mind, but she'd made the right decision. She came to this man she had meticulously avoided all her life, a man who had no reason to trust her, and told him that his wife had betrayed him with her husband. There were a hundred ways he could have reacted. He could have lashed out at her; he could have refused to believe her; he could have shut down, gone into shock, or simply had her thrown out. Instead, they were riding an elevator, determined to fix this disaster before it became a catastrophe.

She was no longer dealing with it alone. She didn't trust him, but she trusted the rage she'd seen in his eyes when his wife kissed her husband. For the first time since she saw that cursed recording, Ramona had room to take a deep breath. She did, and when she exhaled, she felt angry. Unbelievably, overpoweringly angry.

Gabriel. How dare he? How fucking dare he? She gave him everything. She turned a blind eye to his womanizing, to his endless vacations, to his consistent failure to carry out the simplest tasks. She freed him of all responsibilities. Literally, the only thing she asked for was loyalty. Not to her as a spouse—that was beyond him—but to the family that enabled his carefree existence.

She'd worked so hard on this project. She gave it her all, her every waking hour, her sleep, and her peace of mind. She lived and breathed it for the last three years. Her life had become a grind, a constant search for just a little bit more money, enough to keep the project going while overcoming never-ending technological setbacks. The relentless pressure of knowing that if she failed, or just wasn't fast enough to outrun the other two competitors, the family faced financial ruin was her constant companion. It kept her up at night and woke her up in the morning.

The two of them, Cassida and Gabriel, thought they could simply take everything she'd worked for. They thought she would roll over.

Ramona laughed. It sounded like a promise of murder.

"We'll catch them," Matias said, his voice cold like the space between the stars. "I give you my word."

CHAPTER 2

The aerial waited for them on a private landing dock on the seventh floor, sleek, silver with black accents, its lines refined and perfect. A large model, with a walk-in cargo hold, it looked like a bird of prey, designed for precision and speed, a hair short of a military ship. She liked it.

Ramona raised her eyebrows. "A little high profile, maybe?"

"As you said, time is a factor."

Her belongings waited in a neat pile by the aerial: a large waterproof, fire-retardant bag with necessities and a few changes of clothes, a weapon case containing her favorite energy rifle, and a hideous chartreuse gown vacuum sealed in resilient plastic.

Matias frowned at the gown.

"You're going to visit your sick aunt, and I'm going to the wedding of my childhood friend, whom I haven't seen in ten years," she informed him.

"But why is it so . . . aesthetically lacking?"

"It's tradition. The uglier the bridesmaid's dress, the better the bride looks. Also, it's a great distraction. Everyone who witnessed me leaving will remember this monstrosity and little else."

"It is rather memorable. Where did you find this on such short notice?"

It was the dress she wore the first time she met Gabriel. She had worn it in silent protest against the engagement she didn't want. "I have my ways."

He reached for her bag. "May I?"

"Please."

Matias picked up her baggage and walked up the ramp into the aerial. She followed him, carrying her rifle and her dress. She liked the way he moved, balanced, relaxed but ready. The martial art of seco was fluid, relying on speed and constant movement, which was why the secare children started their training by learning dances rather than specific battle stances. But there was a vast gulf between a dancer and a martial artist. Matias moved like a fighter.

They deposited her belongings next to his large enviro-proof bag, which was stuffed so full it would be in danger of ripping if it wasn't made of tear-resistant fabric, and made their way to the cabin. Dual pilot seats. In a pinch, either of them could fly. This was a combat ship masquerading as a luxury aerial. That meant the sensitivity of the controls and the acceleration were a step above commercial transport. There would be a world of difference between flying this craft and an ordinary civilian vehicle. Most pilots would overcorrect and crash.

This ought to be interesting.

Matias activated the console and went through a quick checklist. "The Davenports are the obvious choice."

She'd thought about it too. Like the two of them, the Davenports had thrown all their resources into the production of a working seco generator but had made the least progress.

"And likely the wrong one," she said. "My husband led a rather cushy existence. I take it your wife enjoyed the same?"

"I gave her everything she wanted. Almost everything."

Her curiosity spiked. She really wanted to know what hid behind that *almost*, but his tone told her questions wouldn't be answered.

"Stealing the research carries a lot of risk. They wouldn't have done it unless the payday was worth it, and they expected to survive. The buyer must have promised money and protection."

"And the Davenports aren't in a position to provide either," Matias finished for her.

"Their finances are stretched"—she almost said "even thinner than ours" and then remembered who she was talking to—"dangerously thin. Of course, they're desperate enough to lie to get what they want."

Matias touched the controls, and the aerial soared in a smooth curve. She barely felt the acceleration. He angled the vehicle with practiced ease and effortlessly joined the stream of aerials speeding through the air above New Delphi.

When Matias was eighteen years old, he had left the planet for five years. Her family never figured out where he went or what he was doing, but now she had a pretty good idea. Whatever he did had involved piloting small combat craft and lots of it.

At the time he left, she was fifteen. She'd envied him the freedom.

"Cassida would have done her homework," he said. "She's thorough, and she had access to our database. Our Davenport file is extensive. I trust yours is as well."

She nodded. "So, it's not the Davenports."

"No."

"Still have to check."

"Yes," he said.

"I don't want to hurt them."

He spared her a long, careful look. "Compassion? At a time like this?"

"Were you happy in your marriage, Matias?"

"Happiness is overrated."

"The Davenports are happy. They just had a baby. I don't want to wreck that without a reason."

"And if they had a part in this?"

She sighed. "Then I'll cut them in half. Isn't that what I'm famous for?"

"Very well. We will be gentle as a summer breeze until we have a reason not to be," Matias promised.

"Thank you."

He touched the console, and the aerial swooped down and to the left, banking gently. Ahead the Davenport building rose in the middle of a small park, an undulating flame of orange glass wrapped in an envelope of black callosteel ribbons. The ribbons curved around the building, skimming the solar glass but never touching it, with the widest gap between them barely two meters tall.

At this time of day, Damien Davenport would be at home, while Haider Davenport would be in his office on the twenty-third floor, safe behind that shatterproof solar glass and callosteel designed to hold the enormous structure of the building together through the hardest earthquake. The ribbon envelope was impact resistant. It would take a blast from a midgrade energy cannon to even scratch it.

Twenty-two floors of building security, about a hundred private guards, and several automated turrets. All the standard toys of a successful kinsmen family ready to protect its territory.

Matias steered the aerial toward the tower. "Since you want to minimalize casualties, do you have a plan?"

"How good a pilot are you?"

~

The woman was insane.

Matias gently tilted the control stick, bringing the aerial down another sixty centimeters. He had positioned the craft slightly above the twenty-third floor of the Davenport building, with the rear of the aerial facing the building and tilted just a touch toward it. The gap between callosteel ribbons widened here to make the best of a spectacular city vista, and the rear cameras presented Matias with a great view of the solar glass window and Haider Davenport behind it, sprawled in his chair, his blond head leaning back on the headrest. The man was passed out.

"Give me another twenty centimeters," Ramona murmured from the back.

He edged the aerial closer. A meter from the ribbon. This was as close as he dared to get. Another ten centimeters and the current circulating through the metal would short-circuit the aerial's control system.

This was an idiotic plan. First, she would have to clear the empty air between the aerial and the ribbon, then fifteen centimeters of callosteel, then another fifty-centimeter gap to the solar glass, and then she would have to cut her way through a three-centimeter-thick glass pane, and she would have to be blindingly fast, or she would plummet to her death.

The screen in the dash showed Ramona backing up. She pressed herself against the partition separating the cabin from the cargo hold. Her eyes were focused and calm.

He could just not open the door.

Unfortunately, they had only three options. First, they could ask for a meeting. There was no guarantee the Davenports would agree, and knowing Haider, he would stall as long as he could to gather intel. They couldn't afford to waste time.

Second, he could land on the roof, dodging the cannon fire. They could break in, kill their way down to Haider's office, and get what they needed. That way meant Davenport guards would die defending their employers. He had decided long ago that he was the kind of man who didn't start fights. He finished them, and he never stooped to unprovoked murder. Their ancestors were ruthless killers, but that was six generations ago. Now both he and Ramona were more kinsmen than secare, and the way she wanted to handle the Davenports confirmed what he'd already suspected. Ramona would execute her enemies without hesitation, yet given a choice, she preferred to avoid killing. Life was fragile and precious.

That only left option three, titled "Open the Cargo Door." He hated option three.

There had to be some other way, some method that didn't end with Ramona plunging to the ground two hundred meters below, every bone in her body broken. She was an enemy, but it was a truly horrible way to die. If she fell to her death while he was piloting the aerial, nobody would believe that he wasn't complicit in her death. It would plunge their families into a war.

Ramona took a deep breath . . .

He thumbed the cargo door release. Wind tore into the aerial, but he was ready for it, and the craft barely trembled.

She sprinted, a streak of white, and dived, her arms raised above her head. Her seco blades tore out of her forearms, splaying out like two pieces of radiant red silk. For a fraction of a second, she looked like an angel in white, soaring on glowing bloodred wings, and then the seco field snapped into rigid blades, and she sliced through the solar window and dropped into the hole.

Chunks of amber glass rained down.

He activated the autopilot course he'd programed a few minutes ago, jumped out of his seat, sprinted to the cargo bay, and leaped across the gap. The ground yawned at him, far below, and then he landed on the luxurious Solean pine floor of Haider's office.

Ramona stood with her back to the office door. A gash smoked lightly behind her—she'd cut the alarm wires running through the door, triggering a lockdown. Haider struck at her, a lethal whirlwind with a short sword gripped in each hand. The Davenport family produced offspring with enhanced speed and coordination, and Haider's flurry of attacks was so fast Matias could barely follow it with his naked eye.

Ramona had reshaped her seco blades into circular shields, fifty centimeters wide, and glided away from Haider, parrying his furious strikes in a controlled frenzy. Her shields stretched and shifted with her will, creating an impenetrable barrier between her and her attacker.

Matias charged across the office.

Haider spun to him, alerted by his combat implant, slashing as he turned, but it was too late. Matias dropped under the strike and kicked, sweeping Haider's legs from under him. Haider landed well, flexed, and sprang to his feet to find Matias's right blade pointed at his neck. The tip stopped five centimeters short of Haider's throat.

Ramona plucked the sword from Haider's right hand. "Don't move." Her voice was calm and reassuring. "We just want to talk."

⌐

Haider tossed his remaining sword onto the desk, crossed his arms, and leaned against it. The desk quaked and slid apart. The right half thudded to the floor, sliced on the diagonal.

Haider spun around to look at it and turned back, his face twisted by disgust. "Damn it."

Ramona hid a smile.

Matias glanced at her. "When did you even cut this?"

"On my way to the door. I wanted to slow him down."

Haider stared at the two of them. Slightly below average height, he was built like a gymnast, compact, strong, with powerful arms and broad shoulders. He came from an old family, and the planet had put its stamp on him before he was even born. He was a classic Dahlia blond, with golden hair and skin almost as bronze as hers. No matter what your ancestors looked like, once you made your home in the province of Dahlia, it saturated you with sunlight.

He was also truly fast with those blades, and he'd reacted instantly, going from completely asleep into full assault in a blink. It had taken all her concentration and skill to parry.

"Am I seeing things?" Haider pondered, almost as if talking to himself. "Clearly this is just a weirdly specific bad dream, one where two people who hate each other team up to bust into my office and destroy my prized furniture."

"Bill me," Matias said.

Ha!

Haider knocked on the still-standing half of the wooden desk. "It's old, you savage. Three hundred years old, brought to this planet by my great-great, however many *great*s, grandfather. It's irreplaceable."

Ramona felt a slight tinge of guilt. "It's a clean cut," she offered. "It can be fixed."

A screen on the wall came to life. A harried woman with dark hair and worried eyes appeared. Derra Lee, Davenport's chief of security. "Are you . . ."

"I'm fine," Haider snapped. "Meeting with the new redecorating team."

Derra squinted at the two of them. "Would you like me to send up some tea for everybody?"

A bit obvious for a code phrase.

"I said I'm fine. Keep your goons downstairs. I will expect a full report after this."

Haider dismissed the screen with a flick of his fingers, sighed, and looked at the two of them. "Fine. You have my undivided attention. What the hell was so important?"

If he knew, he was a great actor. She'd have to approach this carefully, choosing just the right words . . .

"Did you pay my wife and her husband to steal from us?" Matias asked.

Damn it.

Silence claimed the office.

Haider blinked a few times and looked at her. "Is he serious?"

She shrugged. "I've never seen him smile, in person or in an image."

More silence.

Haider opened his mouth and laughed.

"Is that a yes or a no?" Matias growled.

Haider shook, bent forward, and held his hand out.

"I think he needs a moment," Ramona told Matias. "I don't think he's involved."

"I can see that, but I still need to hear it."

Haider choked a little bit and kept laughing.

There was no point in standing. This would clearly take a while. Ramona walked over to an elegant couch and sat. Matias remained standing, looming over Haider like some dark shadow.

Finally, Haider straightened. "Worth it. Do you know how long it's been since I laughed like that? It was an ugly desk, anyway."

"I need an answer," Matias demanded. His voice was cold enough to freeze the marrow in one's bones.

"No," Haider said. "I wasn't involved in any shenanigans with your spouses. Let me open a window into my life. My company is on the verge of bankruptcy. I'm reduced to borrowing money from distant relatives I hate and swore to never talk to again. Our precious son, who is now four months old, somehow inherited the Tarim mutation, despite numerous assurances by the best genetic firm on the planet that nothing of the sort could ever happen. That means he could simply stop breathing at any moment until he clears his first year. My husband is the carrier. He blames himself, no matter how many times I explain that it's patently absurd, and he obsessively watches our son every waking moment, and when he should be sleeping, he takes boosters to keep himself awake to watch him some more, because he doesn't trust the best medical personnel our dwindling money can buy. In the past four months, I had to watch Damien, the calmest, most rational being I know, turn into a paranoid, anxious ghost. He doesn't sleep, he doesn't eat, he barely lets me take care of him. I worry about our baby. I worry about my husband. I worry about my five-year-old sister, whom I adopted after my parents passed, because she keeps asking us every five minutes if her nephew is going to die. I worry about keeping the food on our table and salvaging the legacy my family has built. The only time I get any peace is at work, here in my office, when my brain gives out, exhausted by my frantic efforts to keep us afloat, and I shut down into a blissful stupor, which the two of you so rudely interrupted with your unnecessary acrobatics. Have you forgotten how to place a call? Have you considered the painfully obvious method of having your people contact my people, so all of us could peacefully meet in a nice neutral setting? What is wrong with the two of you?"

The office went silent. She saw the signs of fatigue now, the bloodshot eyes, the slight sagging in the skin of the face, and the deeper lines. This was a man on the verge of collapse. Considering that, his response to her attack was doubly impressive.

"His wife is screwing my husband," she told him. "They have the entirety of our seco research, and they've disappeared."

Matias pivoted to her.

"He deserves an honest answer," she told him.

"Well." Haider took a deep breath, pulled his chair from behind his ruined desk, and sat in it. "I am sorry. I know nothing about this. They didn't come to us, probably because they realize we can't pay them. Not as much as they would need to make it worth your combined wrath, anyway."

As she suspected.

"Even if they had approached us, we would pass," Haider continued. "Davenport, Inc., has abandoned its seco initiative."

What?

"Since when?" Matias asked.

"Since the beginning of the month. We can't stabilize the field fluctuations. I can no longer justify throwing good money after bad. We simply can't afford it."

Wow. The shock must have shown on her face because Haider shrugged. "It is what it is. Have you been able to stabilize the field?"

"Yes," they said at the same time.

"I hate you both."

She still struggled with the enormity of the loss his company would take. "Walking away after all this time . . ."

"It's not a complete wash," Haider said. "We've stumbled on a significantly more efficient way to calibrate the

Kelly-particle agitator to sustain a constant flow of energy. It has multiple industrial applications."

He caught on to the expressions on their faces and leaned forward, his eyes suddenly bright. "The two of you haven't figured it out."

Neither of them answered.

"Ha! I have something you don't! You are running out of money. You can't afford to keep researching it indefinitely. You and you are going to pay me for that tech. All the money." He leaned back in his chair, spread his arms wide, and howled at the ceiling. "I'm the smartest man in the world!"

Matias looked like he was considering cutting Haider's head off out of sheer irritation.

"I'll pit you against each other and make you bid for it," Haider continued. "Or, better, I'll want a percentage of each sale. I'll own this planet."

Matias rubbed the bridge of his nose and looked at her.

"Clearly, he's gone crazy with power," she told him.

Matias didn't look amused. The word likely wasn't in his vocabulary. "He's gone crazy with *something*."

"Call me crazy," Haider told them. "Call me anything you want as long as you pay me."

Ramona allowed herself a small smile. Licensing from the Davenports would cost her family a fortune, but somehow Haider's joy was infectious.

"That's a good plan," Matias said. "However, unless we recover our files, nobody will be paying you anything."

Haider sat up, suddenly serious. "That's right. I just thought of something. About two months ago, we were approached for a complete buyout. They wanted everything, every bit of seco data and research, all of the prototypes, even the failed ones, and the offer came attached with a draconian noncompete. Not only wouldn't we be able to ever work on seco applications, we couldn't even utilize any of the side projects we developed as a result. This was 'abandon the family business, take a lump sum, and retire' money."

An alarm went off in her head. "An off-worlder?" she asked.

Haider nodded.

Kinsmen families had spread far and wide through the galaxy. They had come into being because humanity needed a vanguard for its expansion. Their ancestors led the waves of settlers, establishing footholds on dangerous new worlds. Each planet had their own kinsmen culture, but for Rada kinsmen, family was everything. Money mattered less than growing and maintaining the family business, cultivating it, and passing it on to the next generation. Business anchored them to the province. It rooted them, and they grew from it like a tree. Their status, their life purpose, and their self-respect, all of it was wrapped up in family enterprise. No Rada kinsman would ever make that kind of offer to another kinsman. It was an insult, and they would know it would be automatically rejected.

"Do you know the identity of the buyer?" Matias asked.

"No," Haider said. "And believe me, I tried to find out. The pitch came from a private shipping firm, but I'm positive it was only a cover."

"Why?" she asked.

"There was a lot of arrogance. It was less an offer than an order, and when we declined, the reaction wasn't positive. There was no haggling, no bargaining, no attempt to sweeten the deal. We were expected to take the offer on the table, no questions asked. That's not the way experienced businessmen do deals."

The Davenports had a deadly reputation. They didn't actively seek conflict, but if attacked, they retaliated decisively, and they didn't stop until the threat was neutralized. The way the buyer went about it all but guaranteed failure. The question was, Was it ignorance or arrogance? Perhaps the buyer wanted his offer to be rejected, although she couldn't imagine why.

"I can tell you that their cover identities were bulletproof," Haider continued. "Either they have an incredible counterfeiter, or their fake IDs are real."

Which would mean they were connected to someone local with a lot of power.

"Did you record the meeting?" Matias asked.

And that right there was the difference between being born on Rada or off planet. Of course Haider had recorded the meeting. All of them knew it. What Matias was really asking was to see the recording, but demanding access to another family's private business dealings would be the height of rudeness.

Haider stared into space for a couple of long breaths. "I forwarded it to your in-boxes."

Her implant chimed, acknowledging the receipt. They would have to find a secure terminal to view it.

"Hilariously, they demanded that we erase it." Haider chuckled. "You have what you need. Go forth, brave heroes, track down the traitors, and recover your data so you can pay me. I wouldn't recover the spouses, however. Seems like a lost cause."

True, she thought.

Haider waved them off. "You can take the elevator down."

"No thanks," Matias said. "The aerial will be just fine."

He headed to the window. Ramona followed him, paused, and tossed a brief message to Haider's in-box from her implant.

"What's this?" Haider asked.

"One of my childhood friends. Two children, natural conception for both. Both born with the Tarim mutation. They are now five and three. I thought you and Damien could use someone to talk to, and Olivia Solis has gone through this gauntlet."

Haider smiled. "Maybe I won't take all of your money. Just some of it. Happy hunting, she-wolf."

She nodded and leaped across the void into the cargo hold.

CHAPTER 3

New Delphi perched on top of a towering plateau, its glittering skyscrapers and beautiful office buildings vying for space with residential apartments and houses, cushioned in greenery. On the side of the cliff, five hundred meters below the city level, lay the Terraces. Seven platforms, each about a couple of kilometers long and two hundred meters at their widest, they curved from the living rock one under another, like scalloped mushrooms from a massive tree trunk.

The Terraces offered views, shopping, and restaurants, all catering to residents of the city longing for a brief return to the simpler, slower life in the provinces of their childhood. Here service was relaxed, the furniture was rustic, and the food tasted homemade.

Matias touched down in a small private parking lot on the Fourth Terrace, next to a quaint café protruding from the cliff.

Its front wall offered the familiar carved facade of reddish rock etched with acid to a paler shade particular to the Terraces, where any new building space had to be reclaimed from the plateau. A hipped roof with upturned corners, lined with high-tech solar shingles made to resemble blue clay, shielded the building from quick torrential rains that soaked Dahlia year around. The café looked like it had always been there, but he was 100 percent sure he hadn't seen it the last time he'd visited.

The moment he'd swung the aerial from the Davenport building, they'd agreed they required a secure terminal. Haider was a shrewd rival. Even if he planned on making money from their deal, he wouldn't pass up a chance to pry the lid off their servers and rummage through their contents. There was no telling what fun surprises he had stuffed into the file he sent to their in-boxes. If they were dumb enough to open it without precautions, they would deserve everything they got.

They needed a scrubber and a quiet, private location to view their little gift. Ramona told him she had one. Matias had one as well, but if his lifelong enemy wanted to invite him to view one of her safe houses within the city, he would be a fool to decline. Learning more about the Adlers only benefited the Baenas in the long run. You never knew when things like that would come in handy.

Ramona's door slid open, and she climbed out of the aerial. A moment later Matias followed. Sunlight spilled from the clear sky, warming the tiles under his feet. A hundred meters away, the Terrace ended, guarded by a stone rail, and beyond it an ocean of air stretched, the fertile plain far, far below rolling into the hazy distance toward the pale-blue mountains at the horizon. Wind buffeted Matias's face, bringing with it the aroma of cooked meat, spices, and the scent of fresh bread.

How long had it been? A year? No, closer to eighteen months. Enough time for a new restaurant to be carved out of the living rock and wrapped in a facade of Dahlia clay.

The last few months had been a tense, focused blur.

Back when Matias had first left Rada, one of the jobs had taken him down to a planet where the natives raced large, fast herbivores. The animals were used to dodging predators. Despite their size, they were skittish and required small screens on the sides of their heads restricting their vision to the narrow tunnel directly in front of them or they would veer off course.

That's what he was, Matias realized. A Metfost charger, racing to the finish, oblivious to everything else. Except he didn't have a handler. He was the one who'd willingly put blinders on himself and sprinted.

He noticed Ramona standing next to him. She had turned her face to the sky, and the sunlight dusted her bronze skin with gold. Wind pulled at her dark hair. She caught it and twisted it into a bun with a practiced flick of her hand. She looked like she belonged here, on this terrace suffused with light and fanned by wind.

They stood side by side, bathed in scents of cooked food and sunshine. Ramona made no effort to hurry him along. They were in a hurry, but she must've sensed that he needed this pause.

Time was the one thing they didn't have. He made himself turn to her. "Shall we?"

"This way." She turned to the right and started walking.

They passed the new building, then a shop selling ceramics, and she led him to a two-story café, with the same reddish walls and covered balconies on the upper floor under an ornate pseudoclay roof. The thick, scarred wooden doors guarding the entrance swung open at their approach. A server greeted them, wearing an apron, a kitchen towel slung over one shoulder.

"The Green Room, Ms. Adler?"

Ramona nodded with a soft smile.

The server led them past the tables to a stairway, up the stairs, and to the left. They passed through another doorway into a small square room in the corner of the balcony. Directly across from the door and on their left, smoke-colored glass blocked the view outside. Matias's implant told him that the walls on their right and behind them were soundproof polymer covered with a thin veneer of green plaster.

A single table and four chairs waited by the windows. Ramona sat. He took the chair across from her. The server retrieved two mugs of lemonade from the hidden niche in the wall, placed them on the table, and departed. The door shut behind him, and hidden metal bars slid into place with a familiar faint click. A blast-proof door. Ramona had taken "Do Not Disturb" to a whole new level.

Ramona tapped the corner of the table. A console ignited in the wood, painted in silver. She typed in a quick sequence. The dark glass to his left and behind her turned transparent, presenting him with a view of the Terrace and the passersby milling on it. They would still be invisible from the outside, but they would see anyone approaching.

"Nice," Matias acknowledged.

"Thank you."

Ramona touched the console. A narrow slit appeared in the opposite wall, releasing a vid screen showing a swirl of flickering sparks. She had sent Haider's file to it and now the scrubber was crunching through it, stripping malicious code and traps.

Matias pushed a little further. "How secure is this place?"

"The restaurant belongs to the family," she told him. "However, only my brothers and I use the Green Room. I had it built a few years ago, and it's off limits to regular patrons."

Of the three Adler siblings, Karion was the oldest, then Ramona, then Santiago. All three were secare. Karion and Ramona were the closest, separated only by two years, while Santiago just turned twenty this year. Since Karion lost his right arm, he had shifted to full support of his sister. Ramona was the nerve center of the family, Karion was its eyes and ears, and

Santiago was the plasma cannon in the family's hand. When someone had to be removed, Santiago would do it enthusiastically and without asking questions, because he trusted his sister and brother completely.

Sometimes Matias wished his sister hadn't left to marry a woman halfway around the planet. Simone wasn't born secare. He'd asked her once if she regretted it, and she hugged him and told him that the only thing she regretted was that his genetics had trapped him.

"Hungry?" Ramona asked. "I promise not to poison you."

His implant could detect hundreds of known toxins. If she tried to poison him, she wouldn't leave this place alive.

It would be a hell of a fight, though.

He acknowledged the offer with a nod. "In that case, please order for both of us."

She tapped the console, conjuring a ghostly menu, made her selections, and nodded back. "Done."

He drank his lemonade. Tart and aromatic, it was the next best thing to wine when one wanted to stay sober.

The vid display snapped into focus, presenting a list of everything it had stripped from the file. *Let's see, a data tracker, a location beacon, and . . . a worm virus.* Given a chance, it would have ridden back to their home servers through their implants, burrowed in their network, splitting into segments, and detonated like a cybernetic bomb at a time of Haider's choosing, destroying their data.

47

"Haider, you prick." Ramona laughed.

"He must think we were born yesterday."

"You can't blame him for trying."

She waved at the display, and the files melted into a still image.

A conference room with a large mother-of-pearl table assembled from carved barnacles common to the North Arctic Ocean. Three men on the left. Haider, Damien, and Derra Lee on the right.

The three visitors wore similar dark doublets and coordinating trousers, semiformal clothes that could have come from the rack in any New Delphi shop. Standard fare for midlevel businessmen and kinsmen retainers. Three names glowed above their heads: Ronaldo Marner, Weston Lugfort, Varden Plant. All three had conservative short haircuts of exactly the same length. All three sat straight, the lines of their bodies not rigid but far from relaxed.

"Military," Matias said.

"Agreed. And new to the planet. I bet everything they're wearing was purchased on the same day in the same shop."

The recording resumed.

"As I already told you, we decline your generous offer," Haider said. His expression was flat, his stare hard and hostile. A different man from the one they'd met this morning.

Varden Plant, the oldest of the three men, spoke. "It would be in your best interest to reconsider."

Matias focused on him. Tall, fit, pale skin, brown hair, brown eyes. A masculine face. Deceptively middle aged. The galaxy offered a plethora of enhancements and rejuvenation modifications. He could be in his fifties or his eighties. He could be over a hundred, but almost certainly older than forty, because he looked at the Davenports with slight contempt and the impatience of someone irritated by perceived youth and stupidity. Both Haider and Damien were in their early thirties.

Damien Davenport leaned forward. Taller than Haider by several centimeters, he was lean, with long limbs and short black hair, his skin a reddish ocher. Where Haider was speed and explosive strength, Damien projected resolve and staying power.

"We are not interested," Damien said, his voice smooth, almost lazy. "There is no need to argue. We won't be swayed. You have your answer."

"Failure is a harsh teacher," Varden said. "You stand on its precipice, and the galaxy is watching. Take our offer and save yourselves before your enemies rip you apart."

"Oddly grandiose," Ramona said.

And familiar. There was something achingly recognizable about the tone, the words, and the look in Varden's eyes, as if he weren't speaking with human beings but with insects suitable only to be crushed under his boot.

Haider gave an exaggerated sigh. "You've offered three times, and we refused you three times. This meeting is over."

Varden rose, and the two others jumped to their feet, pushing their chairs back. The visitor raised his chin and gave the Davenports a look of undisguised scorn. "I will remember this. In the future, don't blame me for being impolite."

Alarm bit at Matias with red-hot teeth. The world went white for a blink, as repressed memories flooded in.

The recording stopped.

"Not much to go on," Ramona murmured and saw his face. "What?"

"Give me the access code," he told her.

The code to the vid screen flashed in his implant. He connected to his private database, pulled the right file, and tossed it on the screen. The conference room melted, coalescing into rows of soldiers standing still in high-tech silver armor, shoulders straight, spines rigid, helmets held in the left hand. Same height. Same long braid stretching across a nearly bald scalp from forehead to the neck. Same expression: locked teeth, lowered eyebrows, unblinking stares, faces stamped with the need to dominate.

"Who are they?" Ramona murmured.

"The Vandals," he said. The word tasted foul in his mouth. "Star Fall Republic Pacification Brigade."

❧

"The Vandals?" Ramona frowned. "Is that what they call themselves or what others call them?"

"Both."

Kurt's face flashed before Matias, the startled expression on the older man's face branded in his memory, because he didn't want to remember the next moment, when his crew leader's corvette bloomed into a small star on his screen.

He tossed the map of the star sector onto the display, a large sphere punctuated by bright sparks of individual stars. As humanity had expanded across the galaxy, it had done so in bursts. A single habitable planet wasn't enough to warrant establishing an outpost unless the settlers had serious separatist tendencies and could finance their own expedition. Instead, humanity looked for a cluster of star systems with habitable planets in relative proximity to each other. They would identify an anchor world, the place of initial settlement, build the warp gates, and funnel supplies to that world, from which humanity would spread in a starburst to all other planets within reach, forming a sector.

The sectors varied in size. Theirs was one of the larger ones, with Tayna, the anchor world, in the center and twenty-seven inhabited star systems situated at random distances from it. Even with warp gates, it took months to travel from one edge of the sector to another. Most planets traded with their immediate neighbors and with the anchor world, but the longer the distance, the less they knew about the other populations. Only the spacers—merchant marines, convoy guards, and migrant worker crews like asteroid miners—understood the whole picture.

Matias tagged Rada, and the planet lit up on the display to the "southwest" of the anchor world, about midway between it and the edge of the sector.

"Us," he said.

He tagged the other planet, a large world all the way at the upper boundary of the sector, and it flared with angry red.

"Kooy star system."

He zoomed in on it, and the map showed a four-star cluster, with the middle star flashing red while the other three were tinted pink.

"About eighty standard years ago, a military uprising overthrew the existing monarchy and established Star Fall Republic. It's a republic in name only. Only active-duty military or veterans are true citizens. Everyone else is part of a lesser support class with limited rights and even more limited protections. They are ruled by a military high council, and the council's power is absolute. It's as if a totalitarian regime and a military meritocracy had a baby and dressed it in republican clothes."

"Charming," she said. "Is this their elite unit?"

"In a manner of speaking. The Vandals aren't the republic's best fighters. They're handpicked sociopaths, unburdened by morals and trained to obey their commanding officers without any hesitation. To be considered for this unit, one has to have a certain body count."

"So they are killers."

Matias leaned back, trying to push the memories aside. "They are eradicator troops. They are not deployed; they are unleashed. When you need to erase something from existence—a troublesome asteroid factory, a planetary settlement, a military unit whose commander steps out of line—the Vandals are the answer. They have no problem killing their own."

He paused, deciding how much to tell her. Just the highlights. Yes, the highlights would do.

"There was a mining settlement on one of the moons in a planetary system on the edge of the SFR's territory. The miners had settled there a few decades before the SFR claimed the system. The SFR gave them an ultimatum: convert or move. The miners refused to do either. The Vandals were ordered to claim the settlement by any means necessary. It was a dome colony, no defenses to speak of except the settlement police. The Vandals could have simply blown their generators with a few missiles, and the miners would've had to evacuate."

"They didn't," Ramona said.

"No. It was judged as a good opportunity for a field exercise. Besides, the generators were in excellent condition and would have been expensive to repair or replace."

Ramona's gaze hardened.

"Nine thousand people," he said. "Of those, fifteen hundred were children. Slaughtered to a soul. They had a point system. So many points for an adult, a few less for the elderly and children under twelve. Babies counted for a single point. The Vandals kept a tally by drawing numbers on their armor in blood. They had their body cameras, but blood looks impressive, and it was all for fun anyway. The SFR called it the Reclamation and Liberation of Mining Facilities on Opus VII. Their neighbors called it the Opus Massacre."

She stared at him, horrified. The shock melted into suspicion. "Why do you know so much about this?"

Because it irreversibly altered the trajectory of his life. He owed the Vandals a blood debt he could never repay. "When I left the planet thirteen years ago, I joined a mercenary outfit. They avoided the SFR and all its troops like the plague. We were told about the Vandals' adventures as a warning."

Her eyes narrowed. She clearly expected more, but he wasn't ready to reopen that wound. The less she knew about him, the better. He wasn't in the habit of giving his enemies ammunition.

"You're saying that this is a military operation," she said. "The SFR wants seco tech, and they sent the Vandals to get it."

Yes and no. "When a Vandal officer warns you that he is about to be impolite, he means comply or die. If you fail to obey his order, he will murder you, your family, your pets, your neighbors, until there is nothing left but a lake of blood. Haider is a marked man. The Davenports are living on borrowed time. Before the Vandals leave the planet, they will make that promise a reality."

A change came over Ramona. The relaxed provincial woman with warm eyes and lazy movements evaporated, like a kan-mask melting into thin air at the end of a festival. The woman across from him now was focused, her eyes calculating, the line of her mouth hard.

Hello, Ramona. This is more like it.

"Suppose you're right," she said. "Does the SFR have an intelligence branch? Or a diplomatic corps?"

"Yes," he said. "They have a diplomatic corps, intelligence bureau, public outreach bureau, and a few other agencies that deal with the outside world. They're paranoid, and they collect every scrap of information about their neighbors, because they view everyone as a potential threat."

Ramona drummed her fingernails on the table. "Then why would they send homicidal maniacs to negotiate the purchase of seco shield tech?"

Good question.

"That type of mission requires flexibility and a talent for diplomacy," Ramona continued. "Two things an eradicator unit clearly wouldn't be known for."

"And yet here they are." *Without their trademark skull braids.*

A gentle chime sounded through the room. Ramona rose, crossed the floor to the opposite wall, and retrieved a tray of food from a niche. She brought it to the table and set it in front of him. A dish of spicy soup, smoked fish, four different types of local cheese, small fried pastries, skewers of meat grilled over an open fire, still sizzling, crusty golden bread, and honeyed Rada berries.

Suddenly, he was ravenous.

Ramona ladled the soup into two bowls and passed one to him. He drank it. *Spiced just right.* He took a second swallow. *Even better.*

"Good," he said.

She rolled her eyes. "Of course it's good. Everything here is good. They're serving our family recipes."

"In that case, I should have said passable."

"Clearly, you don't value your life."

They ate in silence. Ten minutes later, he was no longer starving, and his brain restarted, crunched through the data, and spat out an answer to the Vandal mystery. He really didn't like it.

"Is the existence of the Vandals secret?" Ramona asked.

"No. Their reputation is an asset."

"How closely are they monitored? As a unit?"

"Not very. They answer directly to the high council and are typically stationed on whatever border the SFR finds most troublesome at the moment. They do not enter deeper into the republic's territory unless ordered."

"Two birds with one stone," she murmured. "Secure the border and keep them away from civilian centers and other military installations."

She was walking the same logical path he took. She didn't have all his background, but she would arrive at the same conclusion whether he helped her or not. There was no reason to hold things back. They had to work together. And yet he hesitated. It was probably force of habit. For some reason, he was irritated, and that irritation made him combative.

"If three men in uniform with skull braids showed up in the Davenports' office bringing the same proposal, their reception would've been exactly the same," Ramona said. "There is no reason for Varden and the others to hide their identity from the kinsmen or to pretend to be Rada citizens."

"They are not hiding from us."

She fixed him with her stare. He imagined a bloodred seco blade unfurling from her arm.

"Why do I get a feeling that you've already figured it out and are now feeding me bread crumbs of data to see how fast I get there?"

"Because I am." He probably shouldn't have said that.

She leaned forward. "Kinsman Baena, you try my patience."

Haider called her she-wolf. Apt.

"Are we working together or not?"

"We are," he told her. "We are temporary allies."

"Then you must share information. I brought you to a safe room. You've seen my people. I fed you. I demonstrated trust."

"I don't have a problem with you. I have a problem with your last name."

She bristled. "And now you've insulted my family."

"It's not an insult but a statement of fact. Our families have been enemies for generations. There is no guarantee you won't stab me in the back."

She gave out a short laugh. "Oh, that's rich coming from a Baena."

"What's that supposed to mean?"

"You have no room to talk of betrayal considering who you come from."

That was quite specific.

"You talk as if our families had an alliance, which my family broke. There was never any such relationship. We were always rivals."

"Don't pretend like you don't know." Her words dripped with scorn.

"I have no idea what you're talking about."

Ramona stared at him, sizing him up.

He spread his arms and stared back.

"Fine," she said. "We have bigger things to worry about."

Oh no, you don't. "Tell me."

"As you said, Kinsman Baena, we are temporary allies. The information you're asking for is outside the scope of our limited partnership. We don't need it to find your wife or my husband. What we do need is everything you know or even suspect about the Vandals on our planet, since they are trying to buy the same type of tech our spouses are selling. If you don't want to share, tell me now so you can stop wasting our time."

Nothing she said was wrong. He had to give her enough information to move forward. The most important thing was finding their spouses and recovering the tech.

He realized why he was being petty. He liked this. Without meaning to, Ramona had rubbed his nose in what he was missing. He would never come to a secret room on the Terraces with Cassida. He would never enjoy a delicious meal in comfortable silence and then discuss serious plans and plots with her. His wife had no interest in sharing that part of his world, and she filled every silence with conversation, meaningful or not.

He also understood that he had to draft an immediate divorce agreement. If he were ever to find this again, it wouldn't be with Cassida, and now having experienced it, he wouldn't settle.

"I apologize, Kinswoman Adler."

Ramona drew back.

"This morning taught me many things I didn't know. I learned that my wife is cheating on me. I learned that she stole our research. I learned that foreign troops have targeted my family, and that my lifelong enemy is the only person capable of helping me. It requires an adjustment."

Her expression softened, and he was struck by the profound sadness he saw in her eyes. For a moment Ramona looked as if someone close to her had died, and then she hid it, and her eyes were once again calm and warm. He was forgiven.

"Apology accepted. This has been a trying morning for both of us."

"Here's what I think. Vandal leadership is planning a coup," Matias said.

"From what you've told me, it wouldn't be improbable. They are already kept apart from civilians and the rest of the military. Since they are used to punish rogue units, they are viewed as outsiders by other soldiers, and they believe themselves to be above other armed forces."

He nodded. "The seco shields would give their ships a massive advantage against other SFR forces. Given time, the Vandals could expand their use to small craft. They would go through the regular troops like a knife through butter. That's why they disguised themselves. They don't care if we know who they are, as long as the SFR doesn't get wind of them being here."

Ramona thought about it. "They would want to acquire all of the technology, everything we have in addition to the Davenports' share."

"Yes."

"But they didn't approach us. They must have changed strategy after the Davenports turned them down. And how did they know we were working on seco fields in the first place? Someone is helping them. Someone local."

"Not only that, but the Vandals wouldn't have taken commercial transport here. They rely on numbers."

Ramona drew back. "You think they have a warship in system?"

"I would bet my arm on it."

"State-of-the-art identification is one thing," Ramona said. "A foreign warship in system is another. They would require a diplomatic waver."

"Which can be granted by a federal senator," Matias finished, his tone grim. "Like Theodore Redding Drewery."

Ramona widened her eyes. "Cassida's father?"

He nodded.

"Wow," Ramona said. "That's fucked up."

Matias drained the rest of his lemonade. It tasted bitter.

"What we have is a lot of conjecture. I'm going to verify some of this."

"No, let me. They are probably watching you. If you start making inquiries, their alarms will go off."

"They're watching you as well."

She waved her hand dismissively. "Matias, let me do this. I know what I'm doing, and I will do it quietly."

He owed her for his moment of pettiness. "Please, be my guest."

CHAPTER 4

" . . . so glad that the artist worked out for you." Ramona smiled.

On the screen Aria Teeling, a short, plump, middle-aged woman in the sky-blue uniform of Orbital Traffic Control, smiled back. "Thank you again. You should see the mural. It's to die for. You have to come over for dinner sometime soon."

"Send me the date." She would keep it, too. She liked both Aria and her husband.

"I will hold you to it." Aria glanced to the side. "And here it is. Looks like Senator Drewery signed off on the permit."

"I'm in your debt."

"Nonsense. Friends don't owe. Oh, and you will love this. It's not the first time our dear senator pushed a permit through for the SFR. He's done it before, seven years ago."

Ramona kissed her fingers and offered them to the screen.

"Oh, stop it. I'm happy to help."

They said their goodbyes and ended the call.

Matias stared at her as if she had sprouted a second head. "What?"

"The New Delphi Spaceport Customs crew leader owes you a favor because you remembered that his father likes Conuvian pottery."

"Yes, I make sure to send a piece every year on his birthday. They are a nice family."

"The assistant immigration court clerk loves you because you helped him smuggle in a foo foo dog for his wife."

"It is an Albine Needlehair Spaniel. They're fierce."

"All seven kilos of them."

"Small dog, big heart."

"The OTC chief cracked a file open for you because you got her and her husband an artist to paint a wall in their provincial home."

"Valina is very busy, and she rarely takes commissions. My mother helped her get her start, and our family is fortunate enough to support her art ever since."

Matias leaned forward. "And now the Davenports may owe you a favor, because you introduced them to a renowned psychiatrist who just happens to have two children with the Tarim mutation and who might save their marriage."

She hadn't realized he was paying attention when she mentioned Olivia's name. "You looked her up. It's not nice to eavesdrop."

He gave her a sharp look. "You're a spider. You sit in the middle of your beautifully woven web and pull the right strings until your prize lands in front of you."

Beautifully woven, even. She wiggled her fingers at him. "Fear my spider legs, Baena."

Matias shook his head. "It's half fear, half admiration. Just so you know, we are partners. I won't be owing any favors to you at the end of this."

"That's the beauty of it, Matias. None of them owe me anything. They help me because they consider me a friend. Being kind to people and paying attention shouldn't be done with the expectation of repayment. I helped them because I could, and it made me happy."

He shook his head again.

"To summarize," she said, "your father-in-law is deep in the SFR's pocket. The Vandals arrived to the system two and a half months ago, and a group of them requested asylum under the Political Prosecution Act. He arranged for their diplomatic warship permit, and he likely pulled some strings to expedite their asylum applications. Their IDs pass inspection because they're real, and according to Immigration, there are at least forty of them in Dahlia, all coded as humanitarian refugees. The warship dropped them off, left the system for two months, and now returned, supposedly to negotiate another refugee drop-off, but most likely to pick up the so-called refugees after they obtain our tech and murder the Davenports. It's not a buying expedition, it's a mini-invasion, and your senator father-in-law is in this up to his eyeballs."

Matias smiled. He actually smiled. It softened his harsh face and lit up his eyes. The effect was shocking. She had to fight herself to keep from staring.

"It sounds bad when you put it like that," he said.

"There is no good way to put it."

Matias rose. "Have you ever seen Senator Drewery's summer home?"

"I haven't had the pleasure."

"I've been neglecting my son-in-law duties. I'm overdue for a visit. Join me?"

"I thought you'd never ask." She got up. "Before we go, do you want to warn the Davenports?"

She said it lightly, almost as an afterthought, and if he said no, she would walk away from him right there. The Davenports were competitors, that was true, and if they were eliminated, both of their families would gladly pounce on their orphaned territory and resources. But that was kinsmen business. All of them grew up under the same sky in the same province, they enjoyed the same food, carried on the same traditions, and laughed at the same jokes. Friend or enemy, they were part of Dahlia. The Vandals were outsiders.

Some things just weren't done.

"I already forwarded everything we've learned to Haider," he said. "I'll call him when we're on our way."

She let out a quiet breath and opened the door for him.

The verdant gardens slid below the aerial, splashed with flowers in every color under the sun. Ramona sighed quietly. If she could open the window—an impossibility in an aerial—the wind would smell of summer: sun-warmed leaves, rich soil, and the layered aroma of flowers.

When she was a child, every summer as soon as school was out, the family would make the pilgrimage to the Adler summer home. Watching the gardens glide below meant the start of the holidays. Two months of swimming in a lake and splashing in the family pool, of climbing trees and eating fruit off the branch, of hikes in the orchards and berry fields that could almost pass for a scary ancient forest if one squinted just right. Long lazy days of reading in a hammock and long happy evenings watching the purple fireflies glow in the warm darkness as adults cooked food over open flames and sneaking off at midnight to catch star flowers when they opened to greet the two moons.

Back then time stood still during summer. Now it was just another season filled with deadlines. They were a week into it, and she'd barely noticed.

"Is something the matter?" Matias asked.

For a man, he was remarkably observant. Or perhaps he seemed so because Gabriel had been so completely disinterested.

"I miss my childhood," she said.

"Summerhouse in the gardens by a lake? Evenings chasing purple fireflies and waiting for the two moons to rise so the star flowers would bloom and release the gala swarms? Climbing a tree to eat the orange cherries?"

She blinked. "I hadn't realized the Baenas' data gathering was so extensive."

"No, I just described my own childhood."

"You waited for the moons to rise so you could see the star flowers?"

"No, but my sister did, and she dragged me with her. Every time."

It made sense. Most families either kept summerhouses if they could afford them, rented them if they couldn't, or chose to raise their children in the provinces. Most children chased the fireflies and ate their weight in orange cherries and raspberries during summer.

Matias smiled. "She didn't have to drag me very hard. I liked the flowers too."

"I miss it. Back then, I thought that when I grew up, it would be always summer. I would do whatever I wanted whenever I wanted . . ."

He chuckled. It sounded bitter. "How long?"

"Since I spent a summer in the province? Four years."

He held out his hand, showing her five fingers.

"Why do we do this to ourselves?" she wondered.

"Family. And the glamour of being kinsmen." His words dripped sarcasm.

"So much glamour. Sometimes I am so glamorous I forget to take a shower for three days and sleep in my office."

"Sleep? What is this luxury? Sleep is all about relaxation. Soft bed, warm covers. I haven't slept since last month."

She looked at him, not sure if he was joking. Today was the seventh. Technically, with the right boosters, it was possible.

"I don't sleep. I pass out, and before that I lie awake making mental checklists, until my brain shuts down and the alarm goes off four hours later."

"Thank the universe you got some sleep, because for a second there, I had second thoughts about you flying . . ."

He took his hands off the controls. The aerial dipped forward.

"Matias!"

He grinned and pulled the vehicle back up.

"If you're too tired, I can take over," she offered.

"I could fly this thing in my sleep."

Sure, you could. "Bad choice of words."

"It was on purpose."

Ramona shook her head and accessed the dashboard display in front of her, pulling in the feed from the satellite. They were about ten minutes out from the senator's villa. She called it up on the screen. A sprawling three-story mansion in the extravagant style of Third Wave, the final mass arrival of the settlers, it was built with pink marble and accented with Cellordion quartz trim that shone with bright crimson when it caught the sunlight.

What an enormous house.

The bottom floor was a massive cube with rounded edges, twenty meters tall and one hundred meters wide, with walls featuring towering arched windows. A smaller rounded cube— the top two floors—sat on top of that huge base, in the center. The space around those two floors was taken up by a beautifully landscaped park. Several curved paths meandered through the greenery and wound their way to the south corner of the structure, where a double staircase sliced through the first floor, leading down to a semicircular pool as big as a small lake. It looked like someone had taken a knife to an oversize three-tier cake and hacked off one of the bottom corners, and the liquid filling had leaked out of it in a round puddle.

Not a single sharp angle to be seen. Everything was cambers and arches, and the dark-red roof was a sinuous curve crowned by a cupola. Everything glittered with red quartz.

"Shiny," she summarized.

"It's meant to reassure voters of his traditional values."

"It looks like rose wine cake. How big is it?"

"Almost twelve thousand square meters."

The average home in New Delphi ran about two hundred square meters. "I didn't realize politicians were paid that well."

"Honest ones aren't," Matias said. "This is a monument to all of the bribes he took."

Wow.

It wasn't just the cost of the house. It was also the upkeep. Even if Drewery automated just about everything, the energy cost of cleaning and maintaining all that had to be staggering.

"Cassida is an only child," she said. "It's just him and his wife in that monstrosity. What does he even do with all of that space?"

"Some pretty amazing things. He has a library filled with antique books. Real paper, vacuum sealed. He has an indoor sports court. And there is a massive atrium in the middle of the house with its own tropical garden, saltwater pool, and an actual sand beach. The atrium alone is six thousand square meters."

She stared at him.

"I'm not joking," he said. "His wife is a fan of the tropics."

The mansion filled the screen. The aerial's camera couldn't see it yet, but they were getting steadily closer.

"Do you have a plan?" she asked.

He glanced at her.

"He is a federal senator, after all."

Rada was divided into provinces, each with its own provincial senate. In addition to that, every province sent federal senators to the planetary council, one representative per each million citizens. Dahlia had eleven federal senators, which made Drewery one of the eleven most powerful people in the province. Only the provincial governor held more authority.

"We can't simply assault him," she continued. "For one, there will be senatorial guards."

"There won't be. He declined the protection of the guard to 'save the taxpayer money.' The guard is loyal to the institution of the Federal Senate. He found the presence of so many eyes and ears he didn't own inconvenient."

"Private security, then," she guessed.

"Most likely."

That certainly made things easier. Still, their approach and everything they did inside the house would be recorded. There was no doubt that if they left Drewery alive—and they would have to leave him alive—he would use the record of their actions as a detonator to explode their families. The future of both the Adlers and the Baenas hinged on what they did next.

She wasn't sure she cared. That thought should have been disturbing, but Ramona simply couldn't muster any energy to devote to it. The pressure she had felt building since she'd learned of Gabriel's betrayal had reached a critical point. She had to vent it, or it would rip her apart.

"Anything I need to know about the senator? Any fun surprises?"

"Lyla Drewery has a combat implant."

Matias had answered without any hesitation. Perhaps this temporary partnership would work out after all.

"I know," she told him. "C-class."

His eyebrows rose slightly.

"You're our lifelong potential enemy, Baena. We keep an eye on your possible allies."

"Then I have nothing to fear. Your surveillance is good, but your judgment is crap. The Drewerys have never been my allies."

She rolled her eyes. "What about the senator himself? Any enhancements?"

"The standard senatorial implant. Combat implants don't integrate well with the senatorial admin models. It's one or the other. He was groomed for the Senate from the day he was born. If you gave him a firearm, he wouldn't know from which end it would fire."

The display flashed with gold. They'd crossed the property line. She could see the red cupola rising above the treetops a few kilometers out.

Two dark aerials shot into the air and hovered, flanking the residence. She zoomed in on them using her display to access the aerial's camera. Not aerials. Gunships. Two short-range space fighters. They didn't look like Planetary Defense.

"That arrogant bastard," Matias growled. "He isn't even trying."

"The Vandals?"

"Yes."

The house rushed at them.

On the display the gunships sprouted twin barrels tipped with calibration coils. A third cannon under the cockpit dropped into view. A kinetic projectile launcher.

"Weapons hot," Ramona reported. "Two Vulcan cannons and a 20 mm KPL each."

Matias whistled. "Expensive toys."

The calibration coils on the muzzles of the Vulcan cannons spun, turning white. When ready, they would fire packets of ionized matter, supercharged with energy to deliver both kinetic impact and extreme heat.

"Calibration initiated," she said, her voice clipped.

Matias showed no signs of altering their course.

They were outgunned. The 20 mm rounds from the KPLs would shred their aerial like a spiderweb. And if it missed, a direct hit from either of the Vulcan cannons would fry their electronics, melt their hull, and cook them alive.

Four turrets rose from the roof of the villa, expanding like mushrooms. Surface-to-air missile batteries. That couldn't possibly be legal. Even for a senator.

"And four SAMs," she added.

Matias smiled. "Such a warm welcome."

"You are his favorite son-in-law."

Her harness clicked, squeezing her into her seat. He'd activated the crash protocol.

"We should land and go in on foot. We'd have better odds," she said.

No response.

The gunships shot toward them.

"Matias!"

The aerial surged upward, gravity mashing her into the seat as it inflated to compensate. The gunships fired, tilting their noses up. The aerial streaked up, avoiding the white-hot streams from the Vulcans, and plunged directly between the two SFR fighters.

Not enough space. They would plow straight into the Vandal gunships.

The world turned on its side in a dizzying somersault. The right gunship flashed by her, a dark shadow outside the window. He'd spun them sideways, squeezing into a narrow gap. The two gunships banked to the sides, trying to turn and retarget.

The nearest roof battery spat blue fire. The aerial dropped under it in a sharp hawk dive. Her stomach screamed in protest.

The azure water of the pool sparkled in front of them.

There is no way the pool is deep enough. We're going to smash into the bottom, and even if he rights it, there isn't enough length to stop in time. We'll crash into the wall. If the impact doesn't kill us, we'll drown.

The aerial pulled up in an almost impossible curve and plummeted into the water at a sharp angle. They skimmed along the bottom of the pool, flying through the water on pure momentum. Walls closed in, boxing them into a tunnel. The proximity alarms wailed, warning that the wings had less than ten centimeters of clearance. She gripped her armrests.

Darkness rushed at them; they angled up, and surfaced. A tropical garden spread outside, separated from the blue water by a strip of sandy beach. High above them, a dome of transparent solar glass flooded the scene with sunshine.

Her seat deflated to normal size with a soft whisper.

The seco burst out of her left forearm almost on its own, stretching into a translucent narrow blade. She held it a centimeter from Matias's throat.

"Did I forget to mention the tunnel?" he asked, his voice calm.

She moved the blade a millimeter closer.

"Did you really think I came all this way to suicide bomb my father-in-law's mansion? The pool outside is connected to this one, inside the atrium. According to our illustrious federal senator, it was cheaper to have one giant pool than two slightly smaller separate pools. One filter system, one robotic cleaning station, and he has plans to turn the walls of the tunnel into an aquarium so you can enjoy the illusion of swimming with the fish."

"Communication, Matias," she ground out. "Try it next time. Before you do something like that again."

His eyes turned warm. He leaned toward her, and she had to retract the blade to keep from cutting his throat.

"I won't let you die, Ramona." His voice was quiet and intimate.

Suddenly the cabin shrank, and she was acutely aware that his presence seemed to take up too much of it. He was still looking at her with those warm, sincere eyes she'd never expected to see.

"You can berate me later," he said in that same voice. "But right now, we need to get out of the vehicle, because the Vandals are coming."

He reached over to the console with his left hand, still looking at her, and the aerial turned around, slid backward, and beached itself, the cargo area facing the manicured jungle.

Snap out of it, she told herself.

Matias's fingers danced over the console without him looking. The cargo door rose, and the ramp slid into the golden sand.

"Show off," Ramona growled and unbuckled her crash harness.

They were fifty meters from the exit when the Vandals attacked. Matias sensed them moving down the curving path toward them and stepped into the flower bed behind a palm. Ramona sank into the greenery across from him. It was as if they had coordinated this without speaking.

The atrium was full of life and sounds. Rare birds sang in the canopy. Small pretty animals from a dozen planets darted through the branches and snacked on orange fruit hanging from the vines. A lot of cover from the bioscanners. But cover didn't mean complete invisibility. At most, it would buy them a few seconds.

Four soldiers rounded the bend, moving in a standard two-by-two formation. Their silver-and-black armor molded to their bodies without restricting movement. It would absorb a shot or two from a typical handheld energy or kinetic firearm, and it would block a thrust or cut from most blades. They carried standard Vandal burst rifles, designed to fire cartridges of tightly compacted pellets. When a single pellet tore into flesh, it exploded, shredding internal organs. When a full load from the cartridge hit at once, it turned human bodies into a bloody mist.

The Vandals didn't value precision shooting. They sent out a wall of projectiles, indiscriminate and deadly.

The front pair of troopers took up positions behind two trees. The rear pair moved forward, covered by the first, the scanners on their helmets painting the jungle in green light.

Ideally, Matias would've circled behind them to take out the rear soldiers first, but they didn't have that luxury. In a moment, they would be detected.

Matias glanced across the path and saw Ramona looking back at him. He gave a short nod toward the soldiers. She winked at him.

They moved at the same time. She stepped onto the path a hair ahead of him. The seco in her left forearm spilled out, turning into a rectangular bloodred shield, while her right produced a long scythe blade. He'd opted for the same shield and a longer, slimmer sword.

The world slowed as they charged through it, too fast.

The pair of troops before them had no time to react.

Ramona slashed, slicing the man in front of her in half.

Matias thrust his blade into the neck of the trooper before him. The seco encountered no resistance. It never did.

Blood wet the paver stones.

The pair of remaining Vandals opened fire. In the split second before they pulled their triggers, he'd shifted both seco into shields and sprinted, aware of Ramona at his heels. The pellet barrage smashed into the double shield, glancing off and mincing the jungle around them, and then he was in strike range.

Ramona spun from behind him with breathtaking elegance, her two seco mutating into wide blades, and struck. Two heads rolled onto the path. She dismissed the seco with a flourish and stepped over the bodies.

He knew it was for the cameras. He had no doubt they were being watched and that whoever saw that on the other end likely wet themselves. But she had done it flawlessly. Every line of her body, every twist, every movement was the definition of deadly grace. Jealousy seared him. He wished she had done it just for him. He wished he was the one to parry it.

Ramona plucked a rifle from one of the dead men's hands.

"The exit is about forty meters down this path," he told her quietly. "They'd be fools not to guard it."

She hefted the rifle and fired into a corpse with a metallic thump. The body jerked, spraying blood and liquefied flesh onto the path as the payload detonated.

"No genetic lock. What kind of door?"

"Hermetically sealed plasticore with a wood veneer."

The atrium was around thirty degrees Celsius, about six degrees above what most people found comfortable, and a good deal more humid. Drewery meant it as a tropical retreat and took pains to insulate it from the rest of the house. Plasticore was a poor heat conductor and therefore perfect for his purposes, but an average firearm would punch a hole through it even with the smallest-caliber round.

"And behind the door?" Ramona asked.

"A hallway about ten meters across." It went without saying that they had no idea how many Vandals waited there.

"Fun." Ramona eyed the rifle. "Do you want to shoot or cut?"

"Cut." It was his turn to take point.

"Then I'll make some noise."

He sprinted down the path. She followed a step behind. He veered right, dashing through the greenery out of sight of the security cameras; she kept going straight.

Matias ran for a few more seconds, then cut left. Ten meters, fifteen, twenty . . . The perimeter path that ran along the wall of the atrium winked at him through the leaves. He crouched in the bushes at its edge. The exit door lay to his left, about twenty-five meters down. No guards in sight. They waited on the other side of the door.

Once he stepped onto the path, the cameras would find him.

A pellet rifle thudded, sinking a full cartridge load into the door. The pellets discharged. Wood and chunks of plastic sprayed into the air.

Ramona fired again, and again, pumping cartridges into the expanding hole.

Thud.

Thud.

Thud.

She was going to run out of ammo at this rate. He had never bothered to get the specs on the Vandal rifles, and he had no idea about their magazine capacity, but judging by the size of the cartridges, they would carry fifteen to twenty, at most.

Thud.

The rifle fell silent.

Now.

He burst onto the path and sprinted to the door. Double thuds of the pellet rifles tore through the silence—the Vandals returning fire through the ruined doorway, focused on finding Ramona in the jungle.

He cleared the last meter and a half. The door was a memory, gone except for a ragged piece hanging from the top. He snapped his seco into two square shields and thrust them against the gap where the door had been.

Three cartridges punched the red force fields and ricocheted. Matias leaped to the side, putting the wall of the atrium between himself and the hallway.

A howl of pure pain rang out. The ricocheted pellets had hit home and detonated.

He dived into the hole, his seco twisting into short, curved blades. Two bodies down, motionless, one soldier trying to stand up on the left, two to the right, two more in front leaping to their feet after hugging the floor. He floated through them, weightless, free of gravity and time, slicing, cutting, severing. Blood sprayed the white marble walls. The last soldier let out half a scream and gurgled on his own blood, his terrified plea for help aborted midnote.

The Vandal in front of him fell. In Matias's mind, ships exploded all around him, blinding flares against the darkness of space.

A faint gasp made him turn.

Ramona stood by the ruined door, the long spike of her right seco buried in one of the bodies. She was looking at him, and he saw admiration in her eyes.

"Did I miss one?"

"No. He was dying. I ended it quickly for him."

"It was more than he deserved."

"My apologies. I'll restrain myself next time."

He remembered her striking on the atrium path. "Please don't ever restrain yourself on my account."

Her eyes widened.

He dismissed his seco and held his hand out. "The blood is slippery."

She glanced at the walls and the floor he'd painted red, put her hand in his, and let him lead her through the bloodstains.

CHAPTER 5

Matias Baena was living death.

She had gotten to the doorway a second behind him. He'd turned that hallway into a slaughterhouse. No, not slaughter, surgery. He'd struck with impossible precision, so fast she could barely follow, and when he'd turned to look at her, she almost didn't recognize him. Everything that was Matias was gone. His sharp mind, his alert gaze, that rare smile that shocked her—all of it belonged to someone else. His face was blank, his eyes cold and empty, as if she were looking at death itself. Not many things scared her, but in that moment, she felt the icy grip of true instinctual fear.

Now, as they briskly moved through the opulent belly of Drewery's mansion, she kept stealing an occasional glance at his face to reassure herself that he was still present.

A duel with Matias would be the hardest fight of her life. She was sure of it.

The hallway ended in a T section. Matias turned left, and she followed a step behind. Twenty-five meters ahead, three Vandals blocked the way. Two held pellet rifles. The third, between them, manned a squad-level weapon on a tripod.

A blast wall dropped out of the ceiling to their left, cutting off the hallway from which they came. Ramona sprinted forward, whipping her shields in front of her as her mind scrambled to evaluate her surroundings. They were caught in a corridor, twenty-five meters in front, fifteen behind, no doors.

The cannon flashed with blue. A sonic boom pealed. The air smashed into her like an aerial at full speed. Ramona flew back and crashed into the wall. The impact knocked the air out of her lungs. Her eyes watered, her vision swam, pain bloomed across her back. The pressure vanished, and she dropped next to Matias, half-blind, trying to suck the air into her mouth.

The Vandals opened fire.

Matias lunged in front of her, planting his left knee on the floor, his right foot anchored to the ground, forming two wide shields in front of him that covered him head to floor. She knelt behind him and thrust her shields above them, tilting them up.

The pellet barrage pummeled seco, ricocheting into the walls. The barrel of the sonic cannon spun, priming for the next shot.

"Through the wall, right, three small rooms," Matias ground out. "Go straight."

Her lungs finally opened. The air never tasted so sweet. She slashed at the right wall, carving a hole in a frenzy, and dived through it.

Behind her the cannon boomed again.

Ramona sprinted through the small room, running parallel to the hallway and toward the Vandals. Another wall blocked her way. She tore through it in a controlled blitz, crossed another room leaping over furniture, ripped into the third wall, and ducked through the opening. A larger chamber opened before her, double doors on her left. Perfect.

Another sonic boom shook the walls.

She slammed the doors open and leaped into the hallway. The fire team was on her left, one soldier's back to her, the other facing her, as the gunner frantically tried to reposition the cannon. She cut through them like a tornado of razor-sharp blades. Three bodies fell apart, bleeding onto the floor.

Behind her Matias emerged from the doorway, his face grim. Blood dripped from his scalp, painting a crimson line on the side of his face.

She opened her mouth and realized she tasted her own blood on her tongue. "Are you okay?"

"I'll live," he growled and turned right.

They jogged forward. Her back hurt, every step sending a fresh wave of pain through her hips. The world was slightly fuzzy.

An ornate double door blocked their way. Matias didn't bother slowing down. Seco flashed with crimson. He kicked, and half of the door crashed to the floor, sliced free of its mounting. Two energy rifles barked in unison. He shifted to shields and charged. She lunged through the door right behind him.

Two Vandals, one on the left, by the couch, one on the right, next to an ornamental chair. She threw her shields up, two long rectangles stretching from her head to her knees, and rushed the one on the right, ripping through the pain like it was a wall in her way.

Soldiers were trained to shoot center mass. It was a remarkably difficult habit to break, especially in the stress of combat. The soldier in front of her was no exception. He'd aimed at her chest and pulled the trigger. The energy rifle spat a burst of glowing projectiles. They sank dead center into her seco shields, harmlessly melting into the force field.

She shifted the right seco into a modified scythe and sliced him from his right shoulder diagonally down, through the clavicle and shoulder blade, through his chest, through the heart, all the way to the sixth rib on the other side.

The top half of what used to be a human slid to the floor.

She used this type of strike as psychological warfare. Cutting someone in half was unexpected and visceral, an overkill nobody could ignore. It also guaranteed instant death. The target didn't suffer. Most of the time they died before they realized what was happening.

Ramona turned. At the other end of the room, Matias dismissed his seco sword, and the Vandal impaled on it collapsed. To her right, Senator Drewery rose slowly from behind a massive desk carved from a huge chunk of ivory.

They were in a large room. Ornate furniture occupied most of the floor, two couches and a handful of chairs resting on a black-and-gold rug. Shelves of polished black wood lined the walls, supporting an array of expensive trinkets: priceless ceramics, awards of glass and metal, congratulatory plaques, centuries-old technological artifacts, and alien insects preserved in amber and crystal. Hand-painted portraits decorated the walls between the shelves. An older couple she didn't recognize; young Senator Drewery and his wife; older senator, his wife, and young Cassida; and finally, present-day senator, a broad-shouldered, large man with a leonine mane of silver hair contrasting with his deep tan and bold masculine features, standing next to a bookshelf filled with antique appliances from the First Wave.

This had to be Drewery's office. The entire perimeter of the room was one giant I-love-me wall.

The senator drew himself to his full height. He walked around the desk, picked up a heavy crystal decanter, and poured a golden liquor into two glasses. She noted the slight tremor in his hand. Her demonstration had had its desired effect.

"You surprise me, Matias. I didn't expect you until Wednesday."

He had a good voice, a reassuring male baritone, and he spoke with the smoothness of a practiced orator.

Matias stalked around the couch. She saw his eyes, frosted over and dark, and fought an urge to step back.

"Today has been full of surprises," Matias said.

Drewery set the decanter down. Only two glasses, not three. *Ha.*

"I see you brought hired help," the senator said.

So, he decided to bet on their animosity. Pit her and Matias against each other, then divide and conquer.

Ramona circled the body bleeding onto the plush rug and sat on the pale sofa, throwing one leg over the other. Everything hurt.

"Where is my wife?" Matias asked.

Drewery picked up a glass and sipped, looking out the window. "I had such high hopes for you, Matias. You seem to have all the right ingredients: intelligence, discipline, a capacity for strategic thinking, a good pedigree, and a background free of catastrophic sins. You lack in charm, but charm can be developed. With the proper coaching we could've made a provincial senator out of you, at least. Yet here we are."

Matias, a provincial senator? She laughed.

Drewery ignored her. "Do you know what your problem is, Matias?"

Matias looked at him, impassive.

"You have no vision. All you want to do is to run your little family business. This province is the limit of your ambitions. My daughter tried so hard to push you to superior heights, but your inertia is simply too great. You will never soar."

"You soared and landed in bed with the child killers," Matias said.

Something was off. She'd seen the extent of Matias's anger. She had expected to have to hold him back once they found Drewery, but now he appeared almost passive. There was no heat in his accusation. He seemed distracted.

Was he stalling for time? Why? A delay made reinforcements more likely. It worked to Drewery's advantage, and the senator wasn't dumb enough to miss the opportunity, which was why he'd launched into this ridiculous speech.

Drewery shrugged. "Child killers, devoted patriots. Our perception of things depends on the way they are labeled for us."

"Why?" Matias asked.

"Money, of course. Why else?" Drewery glanced around his office. "My grandfather was a mayor. My father was a provincial senator. I am a federal senator. With each step, we climbed higher. And each step required an infusion of cash. Politics is my family business, and I am very good at it. Had you allowed

Cassida to broaden your horizons, your child would have been a provincial governor."

Quick steps echoed through the hallway. Cassida's mother marched into the room. Lyla was past fifty, but her face was unlined, her golden tan perfect, and her makeup flawless. She wore a robe dress of pricy spider silk, and the nearly weightless rose fabric alternately flared and clung to her as she walked. She moved like a woman thirty years younger.

A C-class combat implant enhanced agility, reflexes, and hand-eye coordination. It shaved a few milliseconds off your reaction time and improved your accuracy. The caveat was you had to practice, preferably by sparring against a trained opponent. Lyla's life was filled with charitable events and formal dinners, but she practiced religiously, several times a week, bringing in new opponents as she learned their moves.

"You!" Lyla pointed at Matias. "How dare you barge in here! How dare you destroy our house! After everything my daughter had to endure! You vulgar, immoral—"

"Your daughter is an adulteress and a thief," Ramona said. "You have no moral high ground to stand on."

"Be quiet!" Lyla barked.

Drewery smiled.

The rage that simmered inside Ramona flared into a blinding red inferno. Two marriages crushed, the efforts of so many people ruined, just for a bit of money, and the two of them dared to act offended, as if they were entitled to some outrage. She was so done with it. Just done.

"This has been fun," Ramona said, "but I don't think either of you fully grasps the situation. Let me help you gain some clarity."

She rose and stepped toward Lyla. The older woman dodged left, yanking a small, elegant gun from under her clothes. Ramona struck, driving the heel of her palm from the bottom up into Lyla's perfect nose. Cartilage crunched, the impact smashing two pressure points, one in the middle of the nose, the other in the philtrum, just above the upper lip. The secare rarely fought unarmed, but when they did, their attacks focused on knocking their opponent away so they could slice them to pieces.

Lyla's head snapped back. The gun clattered to the floor. Lyla jumped back. She should have been out. Instead, the older woman spun around, snapping a lightning-fast angle kick. Ramona dodged right, but Lyla was too fast. Her shin bone smashed into Ramona's ribs. A blinding flash of pain tore through her left side. If she hadn't dodged, her ribs would have snapped like dry twigs.

Lyla lunged at her, throwing a devastating elbow strike.

Not this time. Ramona jerked a seco shield up. The elbow hammered the force field, and she smashed her right palm against Lyla's ear.

The older woman's eyes rolled into her skull, and she went down like a cut log. Her body hit the rug with a thud.

Drewery didn't move.

Ramona sent her right seco out in a narrow spike, pierced the firearm, sliced it in half, and kicked the two pieces aside. A C-class implant would wake Lyla up in a matter of seconds. Ramona retracted her seco, flipped Lyla onto her stomach, grabbed her arm, twisting the wrist up, and stepped on her back.

Drewery still didn't move.

There, I took out your not-so-secret weapon, and her head is still attached.

Lyla gasped. Her arm jerked, but Ramona gripped her wrist. Lyla bit off a curse.

"Your daughter took something of mine," Ramona said, keeping her tone light. "She can have my husband. That's his choice. She can't have my research. That belongs to me and my family. Your spoiled brat has no right to benefit from it. Tell me where she is, or I will start shaving slices off your wife."

"I'm a federal senator!" Drewery roared.

"I don't give a fuck."

"Do you honestly think that you can get away with a direct attack on an officer of the Senate?"

"I'd start with her nose," Matias said.

"Hand is better," Ramona said. "Hands can be reattached. It leaves them with hope."

"You ignorant, stupid bitch," Lyla snarled.

Ramona twisted Lyla's wrist half a centimeter. The woman screamed. Ramona smiled and released her left seco as a short straight blade.

"New Adra," Drewery said, enunciating each word.

"Theo!" Lyla snapped.

"Cassida is well protected," he said. "We can do nothing for her until we get them out of here."

"Where and when?" Matias demanded.

"The Summer Solstice Festival," Drewery said.

Adra's summer solstice festivities were famous throughout the planet. It started ages ago with a sect devoted to worshipping nature in all forms and over the centuries had grown into a celebration of all things Dahlia. Five days from now, thousands of vendors would line the streets of Adra, offering everything from delicious food and trinkets to lanterns and packets of brightly colored glitter powder to be thrown during the dances. Tens of thousands would dance through the city in a joyous, loud, colorful chaos.

"When did you sell yourself to the Vandals?" Matias asked.

"Seven years ago. They tracked a fugitive to Rada and needed diplomatic permits that would let them stay in system as they quietly combed the planet for her. I pushed their application through the right channels in the name of fostering diplomatic and trade relations. It was a small favor, and they were generous in showing their appreciation."

You greedy slimeball.

"How did they find out about seco research?" Matias asked. His voice still had that distant tone.

"The salvager that sold the data banks to you. The fool snuck into the SFR space and got caught. He told them all about it and many other things to save his skin. My connection to you through Cassida was a happy coincidence. I did try to keep your interests in mind. Initially, I pointed them at the Davenports."

"How generous of you." Ramona couldn't keep the venom from her voice. He was lying through his teeth. "Honesty is the best policy right now, Senator. You planned to rip us off from the beginning. You pointed them at the Davenports knowing that their offer for a buyout would be rejected. You demonstrated to them that you were the only path to seco tech, and then you quoted them an exorbitant price."

Drewery heaved a sigh. "The Vandals are accustomed to doing things their way. Rather than argue with them, I allowed a practical demonstration to take place. It made them more . . . agreeable. I simply bargained from a position of strength. After all, my daughter would be taking the greatest risk."

"I wouldn't classify climbing in bed with Gabriel as a risk. More of a sure bet."

Drewery smiled, and it took every shred of will she had not to slice his face off. "Oh no, my dear. That affair was a month old when the Vandals reached the system. But don't take it so hard. It wasn't about you. It was a punishment for Matias."

"He deserved it," Lyla squeezed out.

"Apparently, your husband turned out to be a lot more fun than the man she married," Drewery said.

Fun. Yes, Gabriel was tons of fun.

"The Vandals wanted our research," Matias said. His measured voice was like an icy shower. "You wanted money. And you wanted Cassida to come out of this alive. Stealing the tech was simple enough. The problem is the handoff. You needed a guarantee that the Vandals would uphold their end of the bargain instead of murdering everyone involved and leaving the system with their prize. As you say, they're used to doing things their way."

"He wasn't just worried about the Vandals. He was worried about us," Ramona said. "He knew we would catch on and scour the planet looking for his daughter and my husband. The easiest place to avoid face scanners is in a huge crowd."

"True," Matias agreed. "And the summer solstice is so well suited for this handoff. No ships are permitted to orbit above Adra during the festival. Half a dozen religions have rituals and commune with the stars on that date. The sky must be clear, and Planetary Defense parks several military vessels nearby to make sure it is so. The Vandals would be cut off. They couldn't simply slaughter everyone and shuttle up to that lovely ship they parked in orbit. The security for the festival is tight. They'd have to fight through it, and even if they managed to escape, the Planetary Defense would cripple their ship, so they'd never leave the planet. You had to sweeten this deal to get them to agree to it, so you offered yourself as a hostage, letting the Vandals camp out here in case we knock on your door while conveniently keeping an eye on their bargaining chip."

"Don't forget the bonus," Ramona added. "Once the research is sold, you and I go bankrupt, while his daughter and Gabriel jet off planet for a well-deserved vacation. Cassida is free and much richer, you are a broken wreck, and I am collateral damage."

Drewery raised his arms. "You got me. Here I am, utterly defeated. You have what you came for. Now do get the fuck out of my house."

Ramona glanced at Matias. He gave her a shallow nod. She released Lyla's wrist and stepped back. The older woman scrambled to her feet, her face trembling with rage.

"Come, my dear." Drewery held his hand out.

Lyla locked her teeth, turned, and joined him at the desk.

"Breaking into my house was a mistake, Matias," Drewery said. "A colossal mistake. I was going to let you keep what was left of your enterprise after the handoff, but I've changed my mind. You should've known your place. I don't need the Vandals or your research to bankrupt you. By next week, your companies will be a distant memory. I'll bury you both and your families with you."

Wow. She took a step forward. "You colluded with a foreign power, you let them into our orbital space, and you allowed their combat troops on Rada's soil. Are you not worried at all, Senator?"

Drewery laughed. "Truly, the naivete is refreshing. The Vandals are here on a diplomatic mission. They have all of the right permits, they enjoy diplomatic immunity, and the men you killed were guests in my home who took it upon themselves to protect their host against a surprise attack. You broke into my home, slaughtered my guests, and assaulted my wife. By the time I'm done, the entire planet will stand in line to suppress you. Make no mistake, I will survive this. You won't be so lucky."

Matias shut his eyes for a moment. Three vid screens slid out of the walls and flared to life, displaying documents.

"What the hell is this?" Lyla demanded.

"A record of your dirty deeds for the past five years." Matias's voice was cold. "Kickbacks, quid pro quo backroom deals, illegal campaign contributions, bribes from foreign powers. You've been busy."

Drewery stared at the screens as if they were venomous snakes about to bite him.

"You're right. You would survive the Vandal fiasco," Matias said. "That's why we'll build up to it by starting with something juicier. Like the Monroe chemical spill. Three hundred and thirty-seven technicians died because the Monroe

Conglomerate failed to follow their own safety protocols. And you absolved them of all responsibility during the senatorial investigation. You literally took the death benefits from widowed spouses and orphaned children, all to preserve the stock price from falling."

Drewery clenched his fists.

Matias pretended to ponder the screen. "You might survive this one as well. After all, you were just the head of the committee, and the generous gift of stock your wife received six months later could be a coincidence. That's why the next day we will follow it with Abbas Orbital Station. In case it's slipped your mind, the Department of Defense used to maintain a reserve of fuel cells on one of Gameda's moons. This reserve was designated for emergency use by the system fleet. You plied the secretary of defense with gifts and favors until she transferred control of the reserve to the Department of the Interior, and then your buddy, the undersecretary of the interior, quietly marked it as defective and sold it to Abbas at a huge discount."

"He's accessing our confidential files," Lyla hissed.

"Yes. I felt that much was obvious." Drewery stared at Matias with naked hatred. "How?"

"Cassida gifted you a lovely vintage Second Wave toaster for your collection," Matias said.

What? Ramona turned to him. "You hacked them through a malignant toaster?"

"Yes."

She laughed.

Matias pondered Drewery. "I knew you were dirty. You wouldn't have offered Cassida to me if you weren't. I wanted to protect my family and my lovely spouse from the fallout when you inevitably got caught with your pants down. While you were grandstanding and your wife was trying to remember which end of the firearm to point at the enemy, I took control of your house and dumped your data banks to a private server. I have everything, Theodore."

"You and I are in-laws!" Drewery snarled. "If you release any of this, you'll get splattered with the same mud. The media will go after you."

Matias shrugged. "But unlike you, I run a clean business, and I've taken steps to guard myself. What was it you said? 'I will survive this. You won't be so lucky.' I've sent the first part to my favorite reporter. She is bright and very hungry."

Drewery grabbed an ornate, heavy statuette of some weird herbivore off his desk and hurled it at Matias. Matias stepped out of the way, and the statuette smashed into the wall.

"Today the chemical spill, tomorrow the orbital station; I'll let you pick the third. We have so many to choose from. You might survive one, but can you survive all of them, and how many people will sit idly by waiting for you to drag them down with you?"

Drewery cursed.

"First, you'll be an embarrassment, then a liability. Your former friends will line up to silence you. One day you will simply vanish. I must say, I'm looking forward to it, Senator." Matias's eyes turned dark, and she saw the shadow of death on his face. "I've waited for this moment for a long time."

Drewery grabbed Lyla's hand.

"Pack."

"What?" Lyla stared at him.

"Pack. Do it now. We're leaving the system." He marched toward the doorway, dragging her with him.

"What do you mean leaving? This is our home. Cassida is here! My life is here! I have a charity dinner tonight . . ."

He pulled her out of the room, and Lyla's voice faded.

Ramona pivoted to Matias. He stood in the middle of the room, a small smile stretching his lips.

"Was it good for you?" she asked.

"The best." He grinned at her like a lunatic and laughed.

CHAPTER 6

Ramona opened her eyes. In front of her, a window offered a view of Dahlia wilderness. Huge feather trees spread whorls of narrow silver fronds. Technically, they weren't trees at all, but giant grasses stretching seventy meters into the air with trunks five meters across at the base. Between them, blue-green Rada evaners, deciduous giants, thrust their massive branches to the sky, each bearing hundreds of thousands of turquoise and indigo leaves. Here and there stranglers flared among the foliage, their distinctive orange leaves and bulbous fruit blazing against the blue-green canopy. Stranglers started their lives as parasitic vines that climbed their host tree to the sunlight, draining it of nutrients and water until it withered and only the strangler remained, now a thriving columnar tree.

It took her a second to remember where she was. Her back ached. A slow soft pain washed over her hips. At least her mouth had stopped bleeding and her vision no longer blurred at the edges.

Ramona glanced at Matias in the pilot seat. She hadn't meant to fall asleep. Her body made that decision on its own. Using seco exacted its price. The secare ate like pigs and slept like the dead, unless they were in enemy territory.

If she told her family who had watched over her while she'd slept, they would never believe it.

The way they'd battled through the Drewery mansion troubled her. She'd fought beside her brothers before. She and her siblings were trained by the same person, their mother. They started with the same dances as children, and then, as their seco matured, they sliced through the same practice targets, and finally, when their family was put to a test by kinsmen feuds, they killed side by side. But there was never the kind of synergy she experienced with Matias.

She and Matias didn't fight in the same way. Their technique differed, but it didn't matter. They moved at the same time, coordinating their defense and attacks without speaking. It was as if they had the exact same instincts.

It was the closest she'd ever come to synchronization.

The original secare fought in pairs. It maximized their survivability and target range. A single secare covered a 180-degree target field in front of them. A pair standing back-to-back covered the entire 360. But synchronization was more than simply doubling the shields and the blades.

Something unexplainable happened when two secare synchronized. Ray Adler, her distant ancestor who'd made Rada his home, called it "a perfect harmony" in his notes. He wrote of a bond, a connection that happened on a seco level that was "stronger than love and family." Even in his time, in the original unit, the nature of that connection wasn't understood and not every secare found one, but those who did became more than the sum of their parts.

It was said that a synchronized pair of secare could empty a dreadnought of its marines and crew in mere hours. Two against hundreds, sometimes thousands of combatants. It seemed almost mythical, a legend rather than reality.

Ray Adler had also blamed that connection for the death of his wife. He left no instructions on how it might be achieved. He stopped short of condemning it, but it was clear he thought his descendants would be better off without it.

Despite his wishes, her family had tried to achieve synchronization multiple times over the next generations. She herself had tried. She always thought their battle dances had to be the key. They were the cornerstone of their training, and she was sure they were meant to be danced in pairs, so she studied them and even recruited her brothers to help. She failed. One would've thought that two secare siblings close in age, like she and Karion, would be the ideal candidates, but none of the Adlers had ever synchronized with each other.

She studied Matias through her half-lowered eyelashes. And here was a secare who somehow sensed which way she would lean and how she would strike.

It wasn't true synchronization. It was . . . killer instinct. Mutual understanding between two predators forced into battle together. Imagining anything more was dangerous and foolish.

He glanced at her. *A handsome man with hazel eyes and a killer's instinct . . .*

She really had to stop. At least she had an excuse for her bout of temporary insanity. So much had happened today. It felt like a week had passed since this morning. Was it even still the same day?

"It's still today, isn't it?" she asked. *Oh, now that was a perfectly lucid question.*

"Yes," he answered.

"Feels like an eternity ago. How long was I out?"

"A couple of hours."

"How long to Adra?"

He checked the display. "About two and a half hours. Might be more. There's a storm coming in. We'll have to swing south to go around it in about ten klicks."

Getting out of the villa had taken some doing. The atrium had an emergency skylight, a safety measure mandated by the government so if a fire occurred, birds and other wildlife could escape. Matias had activated it through his link with the

Drewerys' servers. They'd gone through it at a ridiculous speed, expecting the Vandal gunships to follow. Matias had taken over the SAMs and was prepared to lay down cover fire, but the two sleek craft were nowhere in sight. She had a feeling their pilots were in pieces, either in the atrium or in the hallway. Or possibly in the office.

To both her and Matias, killing was like breathing, simple and natural. Uncomplicated. Slicing through human beings was after all the reason for the secare's existence. Children in their families started martial training as soon as they could follow adults' commands. She was three when she'd learned her first dance.

The act of taking a life was physically easy. The aftermath, not so much. The enemies had been armed and trained, and each of them had ended plenty of lives on their own. Still, she felt uneasy. Hollow and flat. Usually sleep helped, but she must not have gotten enough.

Matias had gotten even less.

She stretched and sat up straighter. "Let me drive."

"It's fine."

"You have to be tired."

"I'm not tired," he assured her in a patient voice. "I'm fine."

Aha. "So, you're going to do the man thing?"

"What man thing?"

"The one where you heroically decide to pilot the entire distance and then be tired and irritable and expect special treatment for it."

He gave her a flat look.

"I'm perfectly capable of piloting an aerial," she said. "I've piloted them since I was twelve years old."

"Who let you do that?"

"My grandma. You flew to the Davenports, then to the villa, and now you've been flying for another two hours. I know you're tired."

He sighed. His fingers flickered across the console, and her own console lit up. She took a couple of seconds to orient herself, checked the plotted course, checked the radar, ran the math in her head on the storm bypass, and nudged the stick, altering course slightly. The aerial responded instantly.

"Smooth," she said.

"I have them custom built." He leaned back into his seat, reclining, raised his arms, and braided his fingers behind his head.

Matias in repose. She wished she could take a picture. Her brothers would lose their minds.

"Have you thought of what happens when we get to Adra?" he asked.

The festival was massive. Finding either Cassida or Gabriel even with the latest facial recognition software would be impossible. They had to rely on human psychology instead.

"Everything you told me about the Vandals suggests that subterfuge isn't their strong suit."

"That's putting it mildly."

His pose was still relaxed, but his expression hardened. Every time the Vandals were mentioned, Matias snapped into battle mode. Something had happened between Matias and the Vandals. Something beyond simply being warned about the danger they posed. He braced himself like a man who had been exposed to that danger firsthand. She was dying to know what it was. But Matias was a deeply private man. He trusted no one and revealed very little, and when he allowed her a glimpse into his thoughts, it felt almost like a gift. A small acknowledgment of the camaraderie they shared as partners. She didn't want to press him for it. It would mean much more if he decided to tell her on his own.

Why does it even matter? Why do I care about what a Baena thinks of me?

"We won't find Cassida," she said. "Most likely her father stashed her away in some safe house filled with his private guards armed to the teeth. They're maintaining a complete blackout, because they know the moment we notice any activity, we'll descend on their hidey-hole with weapons hot and seco out."

"Of course."

"I don't think Varden Plant will be that cautious. He and the other two Vandal officers we watched on Davenport's recording have bulletproof Dahlia IDs, and they think like soldiers, not like spies."

Matias nodded. "The Vandals will act as a unit. They will take over a hotel, some place they can secure, and once they do that, they will start patrolling the exchange site."

She smiled. "Festival hotel prices are insane. People make reservations a year in advance. Forty Vandals applied for the asylum. We killed sixteen. So, we're looking for twenty-four newly minted asylum seekers staying together and paying premium rates."

"Shouldn't be too hard."

"They'll stick out like a sore thumb. Once we find their reservations, following them will be a snap. People at the festival are happy and carefree. These guys will be the opposite of that. We'll have seven days to learn everything we can about them."

He frowned. "I always found it ridiculous. Perfectly reasonable people become tourists and suddenly decide that nothing bad can happen to them. It's like a switch is flipped. Suddenly they're drinking too much and stumbling through dark streets with their implants unsecured. They walk into traffic. They hang off the rails next to signs expressly forbidding it. They think every stranger is a friendly local."

She shook her head. "Matias, do you ever relax? Do you even know what that word means?"

He smiled. "I do. I have even been known to allow myself a sensible chuckle on occasion."

She squinted at him. "My family had you under loose surveillance since you were born. The only time I ever saw you laugh was when you stabbed Drewery's career through the heart."

"He deserved it."

He did. Matias had been married for three years. It must've grated on him the entire time. Having met Drewery, she had no idea how he had endured for so long.

"I'm relaxed right now," Matias said. "This is it right here. You're watching it happen."

"I feel so privileged."

"You should."

"Since you're so relaxed, perhaps you could clear something up for me," Ramona said. "I seem to recall an article I read about a month ago regarding that Monroe chemical spill. The provincial special prosecutor had filed a formal inquiry with the federal government requesting access to certain sealed records. Now why would he do that after two years?"

Matias shrugged.

"The article hinted that new information had come to light."

Another shrug.

"It was you. You leaked it to the prosecutorial office."

He sighed. "It bothered me."

"Matias! An upstanding, conservative kinsman like yourself getting involved in politics. How brazen of you. What will the people think?"

Teasing Matias Baena. Like playing with fire.

"It's not politics. It's justice."

Ramona hid a smile. Kinsmen like them didn't get involved in government. It was a tradition as old as Rada itself. They occupied a special niche in the society, and like Drewery, they recognized that they didn't represent an average citizen. The families lobbied to look after their business interests, and some were related to politicians through marriage, but if any kinsman ever ran for office, they would be shunned by their peers. If Drewery had bothered to pay attention, he would've realized that Matias would never break that tradition.

"Most of Drewery's sins involve theft on a corporate level," Matias said. "He defrauds taxpayers. It's wrong but faceless. This one had specific people attached to it. Families. Children. There were images of the bodies in the file."

"How did you do it? Drewery's server security would've alerted him the moment you copied the files."

"I memorized the contents during a particularly excruciating Rada's Settlement Day party. I've been diving into his server for the last four months during every family function. It was like swimming through a sewer."

"I'm glad you leaked it. What Drewery did, it's just not done."

"Yes," Matias agreed. "It's not done."

A spot of turquoise two shades lighter than the canopy caught Ramona's eye. A smooth dome, crisscrossed by strands of glittering white, all but smothered by the stranglers and obscured by evaner branches. A First Wave temple. They dotted the planet, footprints left on Rada by the failed attempt at first settlement centuries ago.

Matias settled deeper into the seat and closed his eyes.

Ahead the storm loomed, a wall of gray under angry dark clouds. Wind buffeted the aerial. She executed a smooth turn to the south, keeping the storm and the wind on her left.

The aerial jerked. The console went dark. Every system, every display, everything died in an instant.

She looked up at the windshield and saw a glowing hole growing in the nose of the aerial. *Orbital particle beam* flashed in her head. A craft in orbit had locked onto their aerial's signal and punched a hole in its engine with a subatomic particle disruptor, frying all the onboard electronics. The aerial was dead. It just didn't know it yet.

Matias jerked upright in his seat.

She pulled the lever, initiating crash protocols. Their harnesses clicked in unison.

They had about five seconds of acceleration left. If the OPB hit them again, they were dead.

She pulled the stick right, turning the aerial's back to the storm to catch the wind.

"You've got this," Matias said.

He said it like he had no doubt she would land.

Ramona squeezed the last push from the engines to angle the craft for an optimal glide.

The world vanished. There was only the aerial, the wind, and the forest below, rushing at them at breakneck speed, and she floated in the middle of it, attuned to the shaking craft as if it were an aching limb.

A tangle of orange stranglers flared directly ahead. The strangler trunks were mostly hollow. They would break, dissipating some of their speed. She steered for the orange clump.

The forest yawned at her.

With a metal screech, the aerial plowed into the trees.

"Brace!" Matias barked.

The cabin shook, jerking their seats side to side, as if some prehistoric deity were pounding on it with a giant hammer. Branches snapped, scraping against the windshield; then suddenly they were through. Ramona saw the forest floor and tried to pull up on pure instinct, but the stick was useless. The inert heap of metal and plastic that used to be their aerial collided with the ground and plowed through the roots and soil, heading straight for a huge evaner tree.

She jerked her seco shields up on pure instinct.

The aerial grazed the colossal trunk. The impact spun them. They hurtled left and stopped, wedged against another tree.

The seat whispered, deflating.

We've survived.

The red force field in front of her was too dark. She glanced right. Matias had thrust his left arm out, adding one of his shields to her own. He'd tried to protect her from the impact.

Their gazes met. He pulled his seco back into his arms and clicked his harness open. "The OPB."

She released her harness and leaped out of her seat. They scrambled to the cargo hold, grabbing what they could. Matias charged the door, a seco blade spilling out of his right arm like blood. He slashed, once, twice, and the door fell aside. They sprinted away from the craft into the woods.

They were twenty meters away when a second OPB tore through the air in a blinding purple pulse and minced the aerial to pieces.

~

Matias pressed against the trunk of a big evaner. Ramona squeezed in next to him.

Two hundred meters away, a debris field at the end of a long furrow marked the spot where their aerial had exploded.

Subatomic particle disruptors capable of hitting a target on the ground from orbit were expensive and heavy. Most larger military vessels didn't bother with them because at that range they didn't pack enough power. They were precision weapons, deployed against small targets: satellites, beacons, underground bunkers. He'd never expected they would use them against an aerial.

"The Vandals?" she guessed.

"Yes. Unless Drewery bought himself an orbital defense patrol vessel of corsair class or higher."

"That would be pushing it, even for him."

Particle beams left no traces. They wouldn't register on planetary defenses unless someone was in visual range, but the presence of a warship, even one with a diplomatic tag, would. To fire at them, the Vandal warship would have had to drop into low orbit. There was a limited amount of time before Orbital Traffic Control would make them move. The Vandals could stall for a bit, but eventually they would have to return to their designated traffic lane.

"I have no uplink," Ramona murmured.

He tried his implant. Nothing. *Perfect. Just perfect.*

The first edge of the storm rolled across the sky toward them. Lightning flashed, snaking through the dark churning clouds in an electric burst of blue.

Right now, they had bigger problems than lack of signal. In a few minutes, the storm would break over their heads. It wouldn't be a gentle rain; it would be the kind of deluge that made the gardens of Dahlia possible. The forest would do little to stop it. They had to find shelter.

Ramona dug in her bag and pulled out a rifle. "I think I saw a First Wave temple when we were flying."

A temple . . . he recalled being small and standing next to his grandfather, holding his hand and looking up at a bright-blue bubble of precursor transparite caught in a web of silver filaments above their heads.

"Which way?" he asked.

Ramona waved vaguely to her left and clicked the rifle's scope, activating it.

"Why the rifle?"

"Point cloud scanner." She grinned.

The point cloud scope tagged the environment, differentiating between shapes. The temple would be large and round. It should stand out among the trees like a mushroom in the grass.

Ramona hung the rifle over her shoulder and faced the tree. "Give me a boost?"

He cupped his hands. She stepped on them, and he straightened, propelling her upward. Ramona caught a branch, pulled herself up, and scrambled into the crown.

A long moment passed.

"Found it," she called down. "Two klicks. Think it's safe to tag it?"

"Yes."

The rifle popped. Ramona had shot at the temple, and the rifle's targeting computer recorded the trajectory of the round. They would follow the scope the way mythical ancients followed a thread through a labyrinth. As long as the storm gave them another fifteen minutes, they would make it.

Lightning tore the clouds above them. Thunder rumbled, the heavens opened, and the rainstorm doused the forest.

Matias swore.

Visibility shrank to near zero. Matias sliced at the tangle of vines in front of him.

"A little to the left," Ramona called out behind him.

He pulled his feet out of the mud, strode a couple of meters forward, angling to the left, and slashed again, carving a path through the brush.

The forest floor was soup. Mud sucked at their feet and gave way under their weight. The rain had soaked through their clothes in seconds. Warm at first, it felt almost icy now. All around them the canopy shook and trembled, not blocking the rain but channeling it into thousands of streams. If something lunged at them through the brush now, they would never see it coming.

He hacked and cut, half-blind, while Ramona followed him, staring into the scope. If they wandered off course, even by a few meters, they could walk right by the temple and never realize it was there.

His left knee was fucking killing him. He had put most of his weight on it in that damn hallway, shielding himself and Ramona from the sonic cannon, and after that second blast hurled him into the wall, he'd fallen right on it. His back hurt, his head hurt, too, and the crash had done them no favors despite the state-of-the-art crash seats, but the knee would require attention as soon as they stopped and he could get the med kit out of his bag. If he didn't treat it, it would either lock up tomorrow or swell, and he had no idea what the next day would bring.

A wide leaf dumped a few liters of water right down his back. It ran under his collar and washed down his spine. Matias gritted his teeth and kept cutting. Using seco tired you out. He needed sleep and food. He didn't care in which order, but he had to get one of them soon, because his endurance was at its limit.

A tangle of stranglers towered ahead. He ripped into them, sinking into the mindless rhythm of slashing strikes. Cut, cut, step. Cut, cut, step.

A hand grabbed his shoulder. "Matias!"

He turned to her.

Ramona pointed to the right. "We found it."

He looked in the direction she was pointing.

A blue-and-white dome rose to the side, wrapped in a net of strangler branches. It looked like a bubble of pure blue caught in a web of silver filaments anchoring it to the ground. Two wide ramps led to the entrance.

They hurried to the ruin.

First Wave temples took their form from nephri spiders, which laid their eggs into a drop of their bright-blue mucus and wove their webs into parachutes around it to let the wind carry their offspring to new territories. A near-perfect sphere from above, from the ground the temple resembled an egg set on its side, with its domed roof sloping all the way down, like a web tacked to the forest floor just before it took flight. A pavilion rather than a cathedral, a seamless blend of natural and man made, where its worshippers became part of nature without disrupting it.

The building had no doors or windows, only two entrances, formed by the gaps between the roof and floor, directly opposite each other. Matias strode up the ramp, passed under the ten-meter-tall arch, and entered the temple.

The oval building lay empty, its stone floor strewn with dry leaves. To the left, at the widest, deepest portion of the pavilion, a simple altar, little more than a round basin in the floor, waited, abandoned. Opposite it, at the narrow end, a small spring trickled out of the wall into a series of stone bowls, cascading from the top all the way to the bottom, before vanishing into the floor. The blue roof, opaque from the outside, turned translucent from within, and the silver threads weaving over it glowed slightly, sparking here and there with an intense flash of white.

He would have preferred something with four walls and a door, but it would have to do. At least the stranglers had braided themselves over the other entrance. It would cut down on wind.

Ramona dropped her bag and her rifle onto the stone floor. The rain had plastered her hair to head and face. She looked pale, her lips nearly white, and her blue eyes seemed huge and dark.

She hugged herself, shivering.

He had to get her warm.

Matias walked to the altar. About a meter and a half across, it was the same stone as the floor but polished to near glossy smoothness. He circled it, looking at the rim. There it was, a small sphere of stone embedded in the edge.

"I'll be back."

He turned and strode back out into the rain, half slid, half stomped his way to the nearest strangler column as thick as his leg, and knocked on it with his fist. *Hollow. Perfect.* He slashed with his seco. The trunk remained upright, held up by the fronds and vines above. He grabbed it and pulled. Wood snapped, and the hollow strangler broke free and fell, flinging mud into the air.

He grabbed it, strained, and pulled the severed tree toward the entrance. Ramona ran out of the temple and grabbed the other side, and they hauled it up the ramp and inside.

Ramona wiped rainwater from her face. "Brilliant plan. Except it's wet and we have no way to burn it."

"Oh ye of little faith. Do you know how to lay out a fire?"

She snorted at him.

Together, they cut the strangler into logs and arranged them in the altar basin, forming a rough pyramid with the small pieces in the center and larger logs outside.

Ramona stepped back and looked at him expectantly. "I'm waiting for a miracle."

He dug in his bag, pulled out a small knife, and cut his arm.

"What are you doing?" She actually sounded concerned.

He held his arm over the sphere and squeezed the cut. A few drops of blood fell onto the stone. He crouched and pushed the bloodied sphere with his thumb, trying to twist it in its niche. It resisted. He pushed harder. The stone ball turned, carrying his blood with it.

Something clicked beneath the altar. A jade-green flame sprang from a hidden vent in the center of the basin and licked the strangler logs, and they ignited into a warm orange blaze.

Ramona stared at him. "How?"

"It's a nephrytine flame with a trigger that reacts to human DNA and hemoglobin. It only lasts for about five minutes or so, but that's all we need. Fire is a rare part of nature. Water runs freely, available to all, but to harness fire, a sacrifice is required. Technological progress begins with fire, and if one isn't careful, one can bleed the planet dry to keep the fire burning."

"How do you even know this?"

"My grandfather showed it to me when I was young. He liked learning odd things. Look at the smoke."

She tilted her head, watching the thin column of smoke touch the ceiling of the temple and melt into it. "Is it being absorbed?"

He nodded. "The builders didn't believe in wasting the energy. The dome stays at roughly the same temperature year around."

"Fascinating." She pulled a med kit from her bag. "Give me your arm."

"It's a scratch."

"And we're in the wilderness. It needs to be sterilized and sealed, otherwise it will get infected. And after I finish with your arm, we're going to look at your leg."

He gave her an outraged look. "My leg is fine."

"Uh-huh. So you're limping for fun?"

"I said—"

She reached for his left knee, and he jerked away and almost fell over.

"You're being ridiculous," she told him. "If your knee goes, I can't carry you all the way to civilization. You are too large and too heavy. Give me your arm, and don't make me repeat myself."

He held his arm out and let her fuss over it.

CHAPTER 7

The rain kept pouring, unrelenting. Ramona watched it soak the forest steeped in night shadows. Here and there, bioluminescent moss and lichens glowed with faint silver and lemon yellow, tracing the bigger tree limbs. The soothing white noise of dripping water mixed with the crackling of logs in the fire. In this forest filled with rain and darkness, their temple was a dry oasis of warmth and light.

A couple of meters away, Matias slept on the ground under a thermal blanket. She'd rolled hers up and stuck it between the small of her back and the wall. Now she leaned against it, using the cushion to support her aching back. Her whole body felt like one giant bruise.

They had gone out into the rain again as soon as she sealed the cut on his arm and harvested some evaner limbs, slicing them into logs. Strangler burned hot and fast, great for an intense flash of heat but not good for sustaining fire. And they needed to keep it going, or they would have to cut themselves every time it went out.

They changed into dry clothes—she into a light exercise suit, loose shirt, and pants made of warm but breathable fabric, and he into a terrain combat suit that fit his powerful body like a glove. She had done her best not to stare.

They pooled their resources. Matias had managed to grab the crash kit from the aerial on his way out. It gave them two purifier bottles, two days of rations, thermal blankets, portable charger, first aid kit, and field wipes, for which she was eternally grateful.

They'd drunk the temple spring water from the purifier bottles, secured their supplies, and then Matias had stretched out on the temple floor and fallen asleep almost instantly. She was amazed he had lasted that long, with the injuries and that mad sprint through Drewery's ridiculous mansion. She had taken a single blast from the sonic cannon, and the impact had nearly shattered her bones. He'd taken two. When she looked at his knee two hours ago, it was the size of a red peach and the color of one. She'd injected him with a cocktail of anti-inflammatory painkillers and an accelerated healing booster. If he could avoid falling on his knees in the next week or two, he would be good as new.

She glanced at his supine form. He had an interesting face, all harsh angles, devoid of softness. Matias had a resting kill face. Even when he wasn't trying to intimidate, he projected a natural grimness that promised swift and brutal retribution.

But right now, asleep, he was relaxed. His expression lost its severe edge. When he forgot to scowl, Matias was a handsome man.

She wondered what it would be like to kiss him. What would his eyes look like when she touched his lips? If she melted that ice and let out the fire, how hot would it burn?

Ramona sighed. She wasn't in the habit of deluding herself. She liked looking at him and listening to him, she liked the way he thought, and when he thawed enough to show rare splashes of humor, she had a hard time turning away.

She looked out at the woods shivering behind the gray curtain of the rain. Back when she was a young woman, before Gabriel, before the engagement she didn't want and marriage she had to endure—when that Ramona dreamed about her future husband, she had imagined someone exactly like Matias. He was everything she wanted. Competent. Smart. Dangerous. Decisive. Loyal.

That last one stung so much. She could have forgiven Gabriel so many sins if only he'd been loyal. If only he'd cared for her. She was starved for affection. She had pushed herself so hard trying to get the seco generators to production, and now she was running on fumes. What she needed most was a partner she could rely on. Instead, she had Gabriel.

When she looked back at her life of the past four years, it felt grim, a foreboding sketch in black and white. The color didn't vanish overnight. It was a slow, gradual desaturation brought about by small choices.

But right now, she saw color. She was beat up, bruised, and tired, but the world was vivid and bright again. It wasn't Matias, although he was definitely a catalyst. It was the prospect of freedom. The way she'd led her life had gotten out of control. She had to take charge of her own existence. This thing, this mockery of a marriage, which hung around her neck like a heavy weight, had to end. Whatever her future would be, Gabriel would not be a part of it.

Neither would Matias. He was a Baena. That wasn't something either of them could overcome. She had to get him out of her mind.

She'd only known him for one day, anyway.

He'd thrown his arm in front of her to shield her from the crash. *What a dirty move. That bastard.*

"What time is it?" Matias asked.

"A few minutes before midnight."

He sat up, grimacing. The painkiller must have worn off. "Any luck on the uplink?"

"Yes."

He studied her face. "Hit me."

"There is a Vandal cruiser directly above us in midorbit. They claim that one of our satellites suffered a mechanical malfunction and collided with their ship. They are 'performing repairs.'"

"They knocked out the satellite to make sure we don't call for help, shot us down, and now they're waiting to see if we survived."

"That sums it up. The Orbital Traffic Control had put a hole in their plans by launching the replacement satellite, which is why we have the uplink, and they made them shift to higher orbit, but the cruiser is hanging above us."

"Well, it's a good plan." Matias stretched his injured leg and winced. "How long before the OC shifts them to a different lane?"

She smiled. "They have three cycles to comply, or the OTC will board them to assess and repair any damage themselves. That leaves us with a few options. One, we can file a formal report and ask for an investigation to be launched."

"Pass," he said.

She agreed. A formal spotlight on their activities was the last thing they needed.

"Two, we can get ourselves rescued. Your family or my family, take your pick."

"Pass."

She agreed again. "According to my OTC contact, the Vandals are too far out to pick us up with their sensors. Too much biomass and too much cloud cover. They would have to launch a probe, and with the OTC scrutinizing their every twitch, they won't chance it. Right now, the Vandals don't know if we're dead or alive. They've registered the crash, they think we're dead, and they're doing their due diligence. But a moving aerial is a lot easier to spot than two humans in the old woods with a smoke-absorbing temple."

"Which leaves us with the third option," Matias said. "We play dead for three days, until the OTC chases the Vandals off."

"It would be best if they thought we wouldn't crash their party in Adra."

Matias glanced at her. "Why do I have a feeling that more bad news is coming?"

"Janus got back to me."

"The immigration guy with the spaniel?"

"Yes. We thought there were twenty-four Vandal 'asylum seekers' in Dahlia. We were half-right. Drewery had managed to push the second group through two days ago. It took a while for them to process, but they made planetfall this morning."

"How many are waiting for us in Adra?"

"Fifty-four."

His expression went blank.

The moment the Vandals recognized her and Matias, they would attack. They would hesitate to murder a senator's daughter in public, but if she and Matias showed up, all bets would be off.

If the two of them boarded a vessel crewed by fifty-four people, Ramona wouldn't even pause. In the crowded confines of a ship, they would go through any number of combatants like they were practice dummies. At the festival, out in the open, in front of thousands of bystanders, they would be overwhelmed and massacred. The Vandals wouldn't even have to close in. They could just catch them in a crossfire. The seco shields weren't omnidirectional. They could shield their front, but not their back.

Going to Adra was a death sentence. Even if they tried to hunt down the Vandal patrols to winnow their numbers, killing them without being noticed with thousands of tourists on the streets was impossible. And as soon as a patrol failed to come back in, the Vandals would go on full alert.

They could mobilize both of their families. Well, they could try. They'd have to explain that the research got stolen, how it got stolen, and who stole it, and then they would have to convince the families who had been enemies for centuries to work together. They'd have to beg, cajole, make promises, convince, and threaten, all of which would take too long, and in the end they would fail, because Matias was a Baena. If he convinced his family to work with hers, the Adlers would never accept that alliance.

Even if they succeeded by some cosmic miracle, their net gain would be six secare, only two of whom had recent battle experience. It would be a slaughter. And while the civilian authorities turned a blind eye to kinsmen disputes, the moment civilians got hurt, they would have a lot to answer for.

"We need more intel," he said.

"I called Karion. If the Vandals are in Adra, he will find them."

"Will he do it quietly enough?"

She turned her head and looked at him for a second.

"A dumb question," he said. "Forget I said anything."

Her brother would do it quietly. Karion was subtle, meticulous, and merciless.

The rain stopped. The last drops rolled off wet leaves, falling to the ground. The sky turned clear, and above them a universe glittered in a spray of stars. The Silver Sister, the smaller of the two moons, slipped out from behind retreating clouds, spilling a gauze of white-gold light onto the forest.

The temple turned transparent, the blue of its walls vanishing into the darkness. Only the silver web remained, glittering seemingly suspended in empty air. Under the trees, hundreds of rukta flowers unfurled, their translucent red petals revealing whorls of glowing white petals within. A delicate, sweet scent spread through the air. The forest turned ethereal, a magical place from one of the fairy-tale shows she used to watch as a child. She breathed in its fragrance, merged with its magic, and felt herself relax, muscle by muscle, as if inhaling the night air had purified her, purging fatigue, stress, and worry.

So, that is the glory of the temple. We give the ancients so little credit.

Matias rose and came to sit across from her, leaning on the other side of the doorway. He moved completely silently, his terrain suit shifting with blue and indigo as it mimicked the forest. His face was calm. Everything she knew about him told her that he was chewing on the problem, trying to dissect it into manageable pieces. But none of that effort was reflected in his expression.

She wondered if he felt the woods the way she did. If their beauty touched him.

There were only ten meters between them. She could get up, cross the distance, and kiss him. It would be worth it just for the look on his face. But if she did that, she wouldn't stop. He wouldn't stop. They would have each other here, in this holy temple, with only flowers and trees as their witnesses. Nobody would ever know. But they could never do it again.

Why did it have to be you, Baena? Why couldn't she have met someone like him but without the poisonous last name?

The answer came to her as if the forest had breathed it in her ear. She wanted him because he was secare. He was sharp, smart, and thoughtful, and yet when the occasion called for it, he acted without hesitation. On the entire planet, nobody but Matias would do.

She had to say something, or she would walk over there and do something she'd regret. "What's the deal with you and the Vandals?"

130

She wanted to talk.

Matias glanced at her, perched against the wall, her gray athletic suit draping the contours of her body. The light from the fire tinted her right side with warm orange, the moonlight painted her left with bluish silver, and the nearly weightless fabric of her suit shimmered slightly. Her dark hair fell loose on her shoulders, and her eyes were blue like the leaves of evaners. She looked beautiful and alive, as if the planet had exhaled its magic and conjured her from its breath to taunt him. He wanted to touch her to see if she was real.

The woods spread for many kilometers around them, steeped in night shadows and glowing with delicate color. The temple sat within them like a tiny man-made island, and their fire was its heart.

It felt like they were the last two people on the planet, just him and her.

It was a dangerous fantasy. It swirled in his mind, until he could think of nothing else. Lying a couple of meters away from her was torture, so he got up and moved to the other end of the entrance to put more distance between them. Sitting like this, he could still watch her, confident that he would crush any temptation to touch her before it got the better of him and made him move closer.

And now she wanted to talk. They were sitting too far apart for a conversation.

It had to be a test. Life or fate or the universe was testing him, and he wasn't sure he wanted to pass.

He got up and approached her. Five meters, four, two . . . this would do. He didn't trust himself to get any closer. He sat on the stone floor of the ramp, outside the fire's light, letting the night obscure his expression. He wasn't sure what she would see in his eyes.

"An answer for an answer?"

Ramona sighed. "Must everything be an exchange?"

"Yes. Everything is an exchange. Everything is transactional. You breathe in, you breathe out. You train, you get stronger. You do someone a favor, and they reciprocate. You should know that better than anyone, Lady Spider."

"Fine. What do you want?"

Everything.

"In your restaurant, when I told you that I had no guarantee that you wouldn't stab me in the back, you told me that I had no room to talk of betrayal, considering where and who I came from. I want to know what you meant by that."

She mulled it over. "I suppose you'd find out eventually. You have a deal. History for history. Start with why you left the planet."

This woman always went for the jugular. He settled into a comfortable position on the floor.

"My father's death broke my mother. One morning we woke up, and my aunt greeted us at the breakfast table in her place. She served us a hava crumble she'd baked that morning and explained that our mom needed some time away. That she was going to be gone for a while, until she dealt with everything. I remember she kind of waved her hands around when she said 'everything.'"

"I can actually picture that. Your aunt is quite frightening." Ramona shivered.

He imagined himself walking over and putting his arms around her. "My aunt is a lovely person."

"Lovely but frightening."

He thought about it. "That's probably fair. I realized two things, one good, one bad. The bad thing was that me and my sister were included in the everything. We were a burden, like the family, the business, and the house. I never saw my mother in person after that."

It still hurt. Fifteen years later.

"Is she . . . ?"

"She's alive. I get timely medical reports from her annual checkups, and occasionally the villa where she stays requires renovations or repairs. I pay the bills. She refuses my calls."

"Your mother ran away from home." Ramona stared at him, incredulous. "She left you."

"In a manner of speaking."

"I remember when it happened. Our family made a big deal out of it. I was twelve, which means you were fifteen years old, and your sister was seventeen. Your mother abandoned her children. We all thought she simply stepped down as the head of the family. I didn't know . . ."

"Nobody knows outside of a few close members of the family. Nobody wanted to advertise that she'd suffered an emotional collapse."

Kinsmen were obsessed with hereditary genetics, and they gossiped.

Ramona grimaced. "We would've done the same. I can imagine what would've been said if it became public. 'Ava snapped. What if she passed her mental instability to her children? Will they crack under the pressure if you cut them deep enough?' It would be like tying up a bleating lamb in the middle of the woods."

"Exactly. My mother was seen as weak by the family. Nobody said it, but the silent judgment was deafening."

"Do you think she was weak?" she asked, her voice soft.

"I think she needed help in the worst way. With enough trauma and grief, anyone can be broken."

Ramona looked away. "Did you help her?"

"My aunt tried. I've seen the records. Psychiatrists, psychologists, grief counselors, the abbot of the Blazing Mountain Monastery . . ."

Ramona raised her eyebrows.

"Like you said, my aunt is lovely but frightening. Unfortunately, you can't help someone against their will. My mother refused all of it, especially the calls from my sister and me. She wanted to be free of anything that reminded her of my father, including her children. In the end, we could only respect her wishes."

Ramona frowned. "You said you understood two things—one good, one bad. What was the good thing?"

He grinned at her. "I realized I could leave."

She chuckled.

"Until that moment at the breakfast table, I hadn't known it was possible. It hit me like a bolt of lightning. I could just leave. I could just go somewhere else, where I wasn't the son, the nephew, the heir. Zero pressure, zero expectations. So, when I turned eighteen, I split."

"Where did you go?"

"To Calais V. They have a mercenary hub there. One of the crews needed a warm body, so I got hired. They didn't care where I was from. They didn't want to know my real name. As long as I did my job and didn't cause too many problems, they were happy to have me. They liked my reaction time, so they trained me as a pilot. I was with them for five years."

"Did you have fun?"

He leaned toward her, and she mimicked his movement. The space between them was so small now that if he reached out, he could stroke her soft cheek with his fingertips.

"I had *loads* of fun." He winked at her.

She smiled and leaned back.

"I've seen the entire sector. It was a job, and sometimes it was dangerous, but we always had a good time. People who were bad at their jobs died or got fired. Everyone who was left was pretty damn good. I was one of them, and I was pretty proud of myself."

"So what happened?"

"The Opus Massacre. I told you about it. Nine thousand miners slaughtered."

She nodded. "I remember. The Vandals killed the children and marked the body count on their armor."

"Shortly before the Vandals attacked, the colony had sent out a ship, two hundred and fifty passengers and forty crew. Half of the passengers were recent graduates going to Raleigh III to attend the academy there. None of them older than eighteen. Some of the others needed advanced medical treatment, some were visiting family. The usual thing."

The tremor in his right hand was back, but his voice remained measured.

"They joined the civilian fleet in Danube System and sat there for a week until it assembled. Fifteen vessels—four Leviathan freighters, some frigates, and the rest random small fries—all going almost all the way across the sector. Three mercenary companies banded together for the convoy, us and two others. With that much muscle, most pirates would let us pass, so it was easy money. Three weeks of being bored, then a nice payday and a few days of liberty to blow the money."

The tremor was obvious now. He squeezed his hand into a fist.

"We were making a transition between jump points at Nicola. Nine hours of slow flying across a deserted star system to get from one jump gate to another. We were almost to the jump point when the Vandal fleet came out of it."

He remembered it as if it happened yesterday, the wail of alarms and the sudden armada materializing on the screen.

"I was piloting *Wasp*, a light patrol vessel. Basically, a scout ship with a jump drive, two cannons, and a crew of four. For the nine-hour run across an empty system, it was just me and the gunner. We were on the bridge. One moment there was nothing, and then the mass signatures started flooding in. A cruiser, three heavy destroyers, ten frigates. The biggest ship we had was a light destroyer.

"The Vandal commodore sent out a message on the open channel, so every vessel in the system heard it. They wanted the mining ship. Just that ship. He wouldn't say why. 'Just give us the ship filled with kids, and we'll let you pass.' We didn't know about Opus then, but it didn't smell right."

Ramona's eyes were huge. He looked into them and kept talking.

"Kurt Summers, the man who headed our outfit, was the convoy leader. He knew the Vandals by reputation, which was why we were told to steer clear of the SFR. I had him on one screen and the Vandal commodore on the other. Kurt sent out a battle plan over the secure channel, and then he told the Vandal commodore that they wouldn't be giving up the ship. He must've thought the SFR wouldn't take a chance on attacking a multisystem fleet. The commodore said, 'In that case, do not blame me for being impolite.' I saw Kurt's face drop, and then his destroyer went supernova. The screen turned white."

"What happened next?" she asked softly.

"Hell."

He wanted to leave it there, but a bargain was a bargain.

"They tore us to pieces. We were outnumbered, outgunned, and outcrewed. They launched missile barrages, one after another. The first salvo ripped through the convoy like it was plastipaper. Vessels broke to pieces. Drives exploded. Once they crippled us, they closed in and shredded what was left at close range with particle beams. Pass after pass, even after ships went dark."

It was playing out in his head again—the blinding explosions of missiles, the debris hurtling past at catastrophic speed, the SOS calls from the smaller barges as they frantically tried to flee only to be chased down, the screaming over the open channel . . .

"How did you survive?"

"I quit fighting." And there it was. He'd said it. "After the third missile salvo, I spun us around, fired a short burst from the engine, and killed it. We suited up, and I vented the ship.

We drifted off through the debris field, our drives seemingly offline, trailing air."

"You played dead?"

He nodded.

"How long?"

"Four hours. Until the Vandals left the system."

She clenched her fists. "They couldn't have gotten away with it."

"They did. Oh, there was a massive stink. Speeches were made. The SFR was slapped with sanctions and paid some reparations. But in the end, none of the four planets involved in the merchant fleet wanted to pick a fight with militant maniacs armed to the teeth. The SFR makes war. That's what they do. They train for it. They are prepared. The biggest fight Raleigh III gets involved in concerns whose name will be listed first on the latest research paper."

"That's unbelievable." Outrage sparked in her eyes.

"That's what happened. We thought we were badasses. And then the Vandals came through and showed us that we weren't shit. We never had a chance. It was the first time in my life I felt helpless in a fight. Everyone I knew was dead. I came home. I couldn't protect the merchant fleet or people who fought side by side with me, but my family needed me, so I became the man they required. And now you know."

"I envied you when you left. I was fifteen, and I so wanted to trade places with you. I'm kind of glad I didn't."

He looked up at the night sky. "We are sheltered here on Rada. We live in our cozy homes, grow dahlias to impress our neighbors, and have our small feuds. This planet has never known a full-scale invasion by a superior military fleet. Most of us have never known war. I have seen firsthand what an orbital kinetic bombardment does to a city. The moment that salvager showed up in my office with the seco research data banks, everything else in my life no longer mattered. I knew then that I had to develop that tech and I had to control it, because if someone like SFR gets their hands on seco generators, they will become invincible. They will massacre system after system until they drench the sector in blood. As long as I breathe, neither the Vandals nor their parent asshole republic will ever touch it."

She stared at him in silence, her eyes wide.

"Your turn," he prompted. "Tell me why I have no room to talk about betrayal."

Her face shut down. "It's ancient history. It's not important."

"I want to know."

"Matias . . ."

"We had a deal. Pay up."

"Don't make me tell you." She almost begged.

"Ramona, you promised."

She shut her eyes for a second, then opened them. "Have you ever wondered why two secare families ended up on the same planet in the same province?"

"Coincidence? Rada is beautiful." To battle-hardened secare, it must've seemed like heaven.

She took a deep breath. "When the secare unit was made, the Sabetera Geniocracy offered them the Pact. Once the war was over, each secare would get one million credits and one hundred acres on the Sabetera world of their choice. After the end of the Second Outer Rim War, the Sabetera Geniocracy decided that secare were too dangerous to be freed. They went back on their word. They tried to kill the secare, but the unit had advance warning and they scattered."

Suddenly he had a bad feeling.

"The Sabetera was determined to exterminate them. They made a deal with the five strongest secare in the unit to hunt down the others in exchange for money and power. Every secare knows these names, and they make sure their children learn them as well, so the treachery will never be forgotten. The five traitors are Whitney May, Hee Granados, Katia Parnell, Leland Dunlap-Whitaker, and Angelo Baena. Their hands are stained with the blood of their battle brothers and sisters."

He felt a rush of cold.

"The Baena family settled on Rada because Angelo Baena chased my great-great-great-grandfather, Ray Adler, to this province. He was going to kill him and collect the bounty. He fell in love with a woman from Dahlia and chose to settle here instead, but not before he killed my great-great-great-grandmother. That's why when Ray's children grew up, they tried to wipe out your family twice. That's why there can never be peace between our families, Matias."

She rose and walked away into the forest.

⌇

Ramona was troubled.

Last night, he'd waited until she came back. She wasn't gone long. She came in, settled under her blanket, and closed her eyes. He sat for a while, thinking things over, connecting the scattered bits and pieces of what he knew about his family into a picture and failing to make sense of it. He'd studied the family records with due diligence when he was an adolescent. It was part of his mandatory education, taught to him primarily so he could map out the complex interactions between the Baenas and the rest of the powerful families in the provinces. There was no mention of betrayal. No mention of becoming highly paid hitmen or hunting down fellow secare.

There were large gaps, however.

Finally, he went to sleep.

He woke up because she moved. Morning light bathed the woods. He saw her go into the forest again, and when she returned, he heard rustling behind the south wall and went to look.

Ramona had found the terrace.

All First Wave temples had one, a semicircle of stone floor where the outdoor part of the services had been performed centuries ago. The forest had attempted to claim it, but the terrace was raised, and it mostly succeeded in just wrapping it in vines. Ramona must've decided to clear it, because he found her cutting the vines away. He helped. They worked for the better part of the hour in silence until a crescent of white stone emerged, thirty meters wide and thirty meters long. Now she dashed around it, striking at the imaginary enemies.

Matias watched her out of the corner of his eye as she cycled through fight stances. She moved like water, smooth, seamlessly flowing from attack to defense and back to attack again, her seco snapping into blades one moment and morphing into shields the next. He recognized the stances. She was testing crowd-control forms.

He'd done the math this morning while dragging the vines off into the woods. The numbers were not on their side. Fifty-four Vandals. Hundreds of potential civilian casualties. Right now, he saw no way around it.

They needed more information. Until they knew more, there was nothing to be done. He'd pushed it out of his mind, but it clearly ate at Ramona. There was distance in her eyes. She wasn't defeated. He had a feeling Ramona refused to acknowledge that concept. But she was grim and focused, like a cornered animal baring its teeth.

That look in her eyes bothered him. He wanted to make it go away. To fix everything.

He didn't know how, and it was driving him up the wall.

Ramona stopped. "Thirty."

He raised his eyebrows at her.

"If we are caught by the Vandals out in the open, we have about thirty seconds before they flank us and lay down intersecting fields of fire. Even if we charge them, they will fall back, fan out, and take us out."

She picked up her bottle and drank from it.

His own estimate wasn't much better.

Ramona tilted her head and studied him. "Can you dance?"

"Of course."

Dancing was a mandatory part of their training. Four dances in total, each with its own tempo, passed down from generation to generation. It was martial arts set to music, designed to improve balance, flexibility, and timing and to teach flawless transition between battle forms. Enemies who witnessed secare dancing usually didn't live to tell the tale.

"Dance with me," she said.

They were stranded in the middle of the forest with two days' worth of rations, waiting for the battle cruiser above their heads to leave so they could get on with their suicide run, and she wanted to dance. Not spar, dance.

He shrugged. "Why not?"

She turned slightly, left leg forward, right shoulder back, left arm raised. He recognized the stance. The *spinner*. He'd never danced it in pairs. This would require some adjustment.

He circled her slowly, trying to figure out how to position himself.

"You look like you're stalking me," she told him.

"When I decide to stalk you, you'll know."

He moved behind her, mirroring her pose. She stood too close. If he moved his hand a few centimeters, his fingers would skim the length of her bare arm. It was messing with his head.

"Ready?"

He wasn't, really. All he wanted to do was wrap his arms around her and pull her close. The space between them was so small, yet they couldn't touch. None of the dances were designed for touching. They were designed for killing.

From here, they could spin in either direction. "Left or right?"

"Right."

"On three. One, two . . ."

He triggered his implant. They spun right in unison, the fast melody playing in his head. One turn. Two.

Synchronization. She was trying to get them to harmonize and fight as a pair. It was the original way, the art that had made their ancestors nearly invincible.

He could see it now. The trajectory of their spins took them around the clearing in a wild zigzag. If they released the shields and tilted them, they'd become an armored whirlwind . . .

Ramona's elbow swung at his nose. His instincts kicked in and he shied back, avoiding the strike by a hair. She tried to lean right, but his sudden lunge knocked her off balance. They collided and went down, him twisting at the last moment to save the injured knee.

He hit the ground and sprang upright. Ramona landed on her butt and stayed there.

He offered her his hand.

She took it, and he pulled her up, holding on to her fingers a few seconds longer than necessary.

"Never mind," she said. "This was a dumb idea."

"The idea was solid. The right idea, the wrong dance." Matias took a few steps away from her and raised his arms.

She frowned. *"Capa?"*

He nodded.

She stood next to him and lifted her arms, touching her wrists above her head, her body completely extended. If their seco were out, they would have flared from their forearms like red wings.

The fast guitar tore through his mind, music like fire running down the detonation cord. His right arm sliced down and came back up as he turned right. He spun, raising his arms, and saw her glide next to him, her movements identical to his. They spread their arms, bent their right legs, twisting to the right as they thrust invisible blades into their opponents, then immediately to the left. A spike of pain hammered into his knee, but he didn't care. He thrust his arm out, she did, too, and he grabbed her fingers on pure instinct and pulled her to him, spinning her as she came.

A jolt punched his palm, shooting through his nerves. It was the strangest feeling, as if his world suddenly expanded.

Ramona ducked under the glide of his arm, and they stopped and stared at each other.

"So that's what that's for," he said. "That arm extension never made sense."

Ramona's eyes shone. "Again."

They raised their arms. Right cut, turn, grab, twist . . . they came together in the flash. He planted his hand over the top of her right pectoral, she thrust her palm at him, and they shoved away from each other, propelling the momentum into a deadly spin. For a blink they were back to back, slicing at the invisible opponents, and then he caught her arm, raising it up and turning her left. Their backs touched.

The jolt rocked him again. He felt her move, knew where she would place her feet, and caught her as she glided over his extended leg, flexible, graceful, perfectly balanced, back to the front, cutting the phantom bodies on their flank, their linked arms giving her the greater reach.

They broke apart.

He wanted this woman more than he'd ever wanted anything in his life. He knew he was staring, realized that everything he felt was written on his face, but he couldn't make himself stop.

Ramona turned away and walked in a slow circle, trying to calm her breathing.

"Did you feel . . ."

She nodded.

"Is that synchronization?"

"I don't know." She stared at him helplessly. "It's as if the seco recognized each other. It's like an electric shock going through my arms, and suddenly I feel you. I know how you intend to move. I . . . to think that of all the secare in this universe you are my perfect match. We can never tell anyone. My family will disown me."

He wanted to feel it again, the invisible current that bound them into one.

"We need to try this with seco," he finally managed.

"Not yet." She grinned at him. "I've grown fond of you, Baena, but slicing off parts of you to keep as souvenirs would be a step too far."

He motioned to her with his hand. "Come."

She laughed softly and raised her arms above her head.

CHAPTER 8

Karion stared at them from the screen of Ramona's tablet. Matias had managed to rig a makeshift terminal using her tablet and the portable power supply. The signal was weak, but it was better than trying to carry on a three-way conversation via messages through the implants.

They had just finished almost five hours of dancing. Matias's face gleamed with sweat. His hair was damp—he had emptied his water bottle over his head. She knew her own face was flushed. She sat on the edge of the terrace, clearly out of breath.

Her brother raised one eyebrow at her. Of all of them, he resembled their mother the most, with nearly black hair, narrow features, and a dangerous edge.

He glanced at Matias, then back at her. His face remained neutral, but she saw concern in his blue eyes. Ramona hid a smile. No matter how old she was, Karion would always see her as a five-year-old tagging along with him on his older-brother adventures.

"Would you like me to give you two some privacy?" Matias asked.

"No," she said. "We're in this together."

Karion looked directly at her. Having come to terms with Matias's existence, he decided to ignore him. "I found the assholes. You were right—they booked an entire hotel."

"Which one?" Ramona asked.

"You're going to love this. They're holed up in the Kamen." She laughed.

Adra was full of hotels. From small and seedy to huge and palatial, they dotted the city, but the Kamen was special. It was the smallest of the seven hotels in Stone City, the historic district where buildings were carved into the red stone cliffs.

The screen split, and the Kamen appeared on the right side. The front wall of the hotel emerged from the living rock of a towering mountain, fifty meters tall and consisting of three oversize floors. Ornate columns flanked the two entrances and rose high to hug a third-floor balcony large enough to host a small wedding. Those entrances were the only way in or out of the hotel. Everything except the front facade was blocked by the mountain.

Two walls, each thirty-two meters tall and six meters wide, thrust from the sides of the hotel, cut into the mountain. A stone plaza lay between them. Each of the seven Stone City hotels faced one, flanked on the sides by tall walls. During the festival, the plazas hosted the dances, a different dance for each hotel. Dancing groups made their circuit, moving from one location to the next, while tourists watched them from the walls and VIPs viewed their performances from hotel balconies cut into the living rock.

The Kamen was an easy place to defend and a horrible place to escape from. It was also in high demand during the festival, booked months in advance.

"How the hell did they book the entire place?" she wondered.

Karion looked at Matias.

"Drewery." Matias spat out the name like it tasted rotten.

"He made some sort of deal with the owners. They canceled all reservations, citing 'state needs.' They're likely regretting it now, since the senator's dirty laundry is being aired over every news channel. Two Senate investigations have been announced."

"The Vandals must have paid an exorbitant amount for the hotel," she guessed.

Matias leaned forward. "Did they book the walls?"

Karion kept looking at her. "The Kamen is privately owned, but the walls belong to the city. Those spots were booked directly through Adra's festival commission. Some of them were awarded as prizes for cultural achievements and contributions to the city. Drewery couldn't touch them."

Her brother allowed himself a narrow predatory smile. "It gets better. During the festival the two tunnels leading to the walls to the hotel are closed. The spectators have to enter from the street via a staircase, and the city's security forces keep the foot traffic out. Unless you're on the list, you're not getting on those walls."

That meant no Vandals would be shooting at them from the top of the walls.

"However, there are sitting galleries on both sides of the plaza, on the ground level," Karion continued. "They are reserved for guests of the hotel. If you enter that plaza, you will be fired upon from both sides and the hotel itself. It will be a killing box."

"Can we get a spot on the walls?" Ramona asked.

"Are you worried about the spectators?" Karion asked.

"I'm worried that the Vandals will try to shoot their way to higher ground once we start killing them. The city's security is expecting drunk tourists trying to crash the party and dance with the pretty people. They're not prepared for mass murderers in combat armor carrying burst rifles. I want to put someone on those staircases."

For all his perceived power, Drewery was not a kinsman. The provinces ran on favors, and the old kinsmen families had a lot of influence.

Karion rubbed his face, thinking. "Uncle Sabor would be your best bet. He should have enough clout, but he'd only do it if you asked him."

"I'll make the call," she told him.

"I think you should reconsider this plan," Karion said. "The risk is too high."

"We don't have a choice," Ramona said. "We must recover the tech, and hitting them at the hotel is the only way to minimize casualties."

Her brother glanced at Matias.

"Just say it," she said.

"There are fifty-four Vandal 'asylum seekers' staying at the Kamen. And an off-worlder."

Suddenly she was uneasy. "Name?"

"Lukas Dunlap-Whitaker."

The name lashed her like a whip.

Matias clenched his jaw for a moment, the line of his mouth hard. "Varden got himself a pet secare."

Karion ignored him. "Lukas lists himself as a mercenary. He isn't. He is a killer for hire. He's been doing this for forty years, and he's very good at it. Two hundred and twelve confirmed kills to his name. Four of them secare. He actively looks for secare jobs. He likes eliminating us."

Damn it. "Thank you," she said.

"Think about it carefully. You remember what Ray wrote in his notes."

"Ray wrote a lot of things," she said.

"'The secare are wolves who know only war and murder,'" Karion quoted. "We are not wolves, Ramona. We are dogs. We still bite and rip, but only when we have to, because we made a nice life for ourselves on this planet. That man is a wolf. Some things are not worth dying for. I sent you the roster of the guests on the wall. I'll wait for your decision."

Her brother touched his fingertips to his lips, brushed his forehead, and the screen went dark.

She checked the file through her implant, looking at a row of spectator names. *Damn.* She closed her eyes for a long moment. There was no way to win. Everything she had worked so hard for was teetering on the edge of a cliff, and she didn't know how to keep it from falling.

"Talk to me," Matias said.

"First, we still have the issue of civilian casualties. How many people have you killed, Matias? I'm not talking about when you were in space. How many people have you killed on Rada, with your seco?"

"Counting the Vandals?"

"Yes."

"Twenty-four. Two in an isolated incident of industrial espionage, another three because an idiot decided to make his name by attacking me in public and his bodyguards jumped in, and the rest of the people I killed during the feud with the Vinogradov clan. They tested me after I took over the family."

"Thirty-one for me. You were expected to take over the Baena family. The attack on you was almost a courtesy. I was seen as a last-minute replacement for Karion. I was tested twice, first by the Rook Trust and then by the Le family. Every life I ever took was in self-defense or retaliation, and even so, I've killed enough people for a lifetime already. I don't want to accidentally hurt an innocent person. I don't want anyone to be caught in a crossfire. I can't. It's not worth it."

He crouched by her. "I know. I understand."

"And, we've been trying to do this quietly, and there will be nothing quiet about this. I've looked at the roster of guests. Adra's mayor will be on those walls. Park Sung Hyo, the provincial senator. Three kinsmen families . . . there will be no way to hide that we were dumb enough to let our spouses have an affair and run away together with our research. Everyone will know."

"Perhaps that's not a bad thing."

She frowned at him. "How? Even if we win by some miracle, our standing in society will be disintegrated. That means more feuds, more blood."

"Right now, there are foreign troops on the soil of this planet, brought here by a corrupt senator. They have threatened Rada's citizens, attacked them, and now they are planning to purchase tech stolen from two kinsmen families. If it wasn't us, if it was the Escanas, or the Vinogradovs, or any other kinsmen family, and you knew they were about to face off with the Vandals, would you help them?"

"Of course. We are all Dahlia kinsmen."

"Would they earn your respect, even though they had been betrayed by people they trusted?"

"Yes."

He smiled at her. "It's Adra. Everyone appreciates a good show. Dancing in Kamen Plaza or two kinsmen secare taking back their property and honor from the foreign eradicator troops. Which show would you rather watch if you were Adra's mayor?"

A faint light appeared at the end of the dark tunnel in her head. She started toward it. "We'll get points for style, if nothing else."

"It's not the betrayal," Matias said. "It's how we handle it. It's our mess. Hiding it is no longer an option, so we will take care of it in front of everyone. We do not hide, we do not sneak—we do it, and we make sure nobody who watches it ever forgets it."

Ramona smiled.

Matias stretched, rubbing his knee. The healing booster had taken care of the swelling and most of the pain, leaving behind only an echo of a dull ache. It was their fourth evening in the forest. Tomorrow his people would pick them up. They'd have twenty-four hours to prep in Adra. The plan was complicated. He would have liked two weeks to test it, but even then, he couldn't recreate battle conditions. It would either work or it wouldn't.

He had called his aunt after Karion had told them about the secare. He asked for a favor, and then he asked about Angelo Baena.

"The girl told you," Nadira had said. "Well, she is a secare. She knows where to stab."

"Is it true?"

"Yes."

"Why didn't anyone tell me?"

"Blame your great-grandfather," she told him. "After that second clash, he purged all of the records. He didn't want the future generations to grow up with the family's shame. I only know because he had forgotten about some data banks he left in an old storage room, and I found them when I was about twelve. It rocked my world. My father didn't even know."

"You should've told me."

"What would it have accomplished? Angelo Baena wasn't some heartless renegade, Matias. He did what he did because he was part of a synchronized pair, and when their unit withdrew from one of the final battles, they left him and the woman he loved behind. They abandoned them to their fate, Matias. He survived; she did not. His diary will make your soul bleed. He didn't want money. He wanted revenge. He stopped because he had done to Ray Adler the exact same thing Ray Adler had done to him, and it didn't make him feel any better. He regretted it every day of his life. It's ancient history. Let it go."

"It would feel like you're torn in two."

"What?"

"Losing your match in a pair. Like having half of you amputated."

She'd stared at him with her piercing eyes. "Did you and the Adler girl synchronize?"

He hesitated for half a second. It felt like betraying Ramona's confidence, like sharing something that belonged only to the two of them. But sooner or later their families would have to know, because he had no intention of letting Ramona go. "Yes."

Nadira glared at him. She was the closest person to a mother he'd had ever since his own parent abandoned him. Being on the receiving end of that stare was like hurtling into the sun.

"Are you sure?"

"Yes."

"Six generations since the last synchronization, and you pair up with your lifelong enemy?"

Lifelong enemy was a bit of a stretch, but he didn't want to argue. "Yes."

Nadira stared at him for another long moment. "Why can't anything be simple with you, Matias?"

"Because life is complicated."

She'd exhaled and waved him off. "Go. Practice. Work on achieving harmony. I need to pray."

He did practice, until he thought his body would give out. And after he was done, he made himself work on things that would have to be settled tomorrow, because he didn't want to think about turning into Angelo Baena.

Matias looked away from the divorce agreement on the tablet in front of him. The sun had set a while ago. Around them the forest breathed. Swarms of purple fireflies meandered through the air, mesmerizing spots of light against the indigo and navy of the woods. It was beautiful in the way only the wilderness untouched by humans could be.

He glanced at Ramona perched on the ramp of the temple. She bent over her own tablet. Her dark hair was loose, and it spilled over her shoulder in a soft curtain.

They needed more training. They needed more time.

She looked up as if sensing his stare. He wiggled the tablet at her. "I'll show you mine if you show me yours."

She passed her tablet to him without a smile.

He looked at it. "An annulment? After four years?"

"He will give it to me." Steel vibrated in her voice.

"Why not a divorce?"

"A divorce is when two people can't make their partnership work. We were never partners."

He gave the tablet back to her. "Tell me about him."

She looked up at the night sky. "Gabriel is a quintessential 'second son.' His family owns a freight fleet. His grandfather built it, his father improved it, his older cousin runs it. She runs it well, very well. Five years ago, Gabriel's older brother tried to stage a family coup. He felt he had a better claim than his cousin. Their father picked his cousin as his successor for a reason, and when Gabriel's brother took off with a third of their fleet, she asked my father to solve her problem. In the secare way."

"Did he?" Matias already knew the answer, but he wanted to hear her say it.

"Yes. My father would never accept money for his services."

"Only the traitors do mercenary work," he said.

She sighed. "You're not a traitor, Matias. Angelo Baena was, but you are not him. Anyway, my father trades favors. In this case, it was an exceptionally large favor, and he wanted an equally significant favor in return. Rada had to become a permanent stop on their trade route, and our family would be guaranteed a cargo spot on any of their vessels stopping here, no questions asked, at a very steep discount. They agreed on condition that I marry Gabriel, conveniently taking him out of the picture before someone in their family decided to use him for a second coup."

"What was your father shipping?"

Ramona gave him a side-eye. "Wouldn't you like to know."

"The tax on exporting relucyte relays is thirty percent," Matias said. "It's quite prohibitive. Of course, your father couldn't possibly be shipping relucyte. That would make him a dirty tax evader. What were those shipments labeled? Oh, I remember now. Low-grade transistor modifiers."

She picked up a pebble and tossed it at him.

"Was it worth it?" he asked.

"No. I didn't want to marry Gabriel, but Father threatened to excise me, and he was stubborn enough to go through with it. Karion had just lost his arm, and Santiago kept getting into dumb fights and creating legal issues. I had to stay. A year later I forced my father out."

He thought her father had peacefully retired. "How did you manage that?"

"I had help from my mother. She'd wanted to retire for a long time. And my father didn't resist very much. He was in his late fifties when he had us. By the time I took over, he had worked on behalf of the family for seventy-two years. The day after he retired, we were out of the relucyte business."

"How did he take it?"

"Surprisingly well. He believed in trial by fire. In ancient times, my father would have thrown me and my brothers in a pit with wolves to fight over scraps to toughen us up. He later told me that I had been too passive. Forcing me into a marriage

I hated 'galvanized' me into action. When I had gotten the better of him, it just confirmed in his head that he had done everything right. The relucyte was no longer his problem. He settled into his forced retirement. Occasionally he calls me and nags me about producing some grandchildren."

"Why didn't you have any? You like children."

"I didn't want to have Gabriel's children."

The finality in her words struck at him.

"It's not because he didn't want to. Gabriel would have loved to have a little version of himself. It was a punishment."

Inwardly, Matias recoiled. He'd never understood why he and Cassida were childless. They'd slept together often enough, at least in the first two years. Neither of them was infertile. Now he knew. Cassida didn't want to have his children. She had written him off.

"What kind of man is Gabriel?" he asked.

Ramona sighed again. "Charming. He is easy to talk to. He'll greet you with a welcoming and genuine smile. He makes you feel like he's really glad to see you and very interested in whatever you have to say. You'll talk to him for fifteen minutes, and half an hour later you can't recall exactly what you've discussed, but you'll be left with this vague pleasant feeling. And if somebody asks you about him, you'll tell them Gabriel is the nicest guy."

That explained volumes.

"At first I tried giving him a position with the family. Nothing too important, but enough to keep him busy. He had a nice office and his own team. He played businessman for about three months. He was openly distracted during meetings, he forced his subordinates to make decisions for him, and he gave his team no direction, but he charmed the four female employees into his bed. One of them was almost three times my age."

"Why?" *Why would a man married to Ramona be with anyone else?*

"Because he could. Cheating is pathological with him. I quietly replaced him and told him to direct his attention away from the family's employees. Having your husband screwing everybody who works for you tends to damage one's standing."

He knew kinsmen who would've killed for less. "Did he ever try to justify it?"

She shook her head. "He didn't feel he had to. The first time, when I was angry and hurt, he waited until I vented enough, gave me that charming smile, and told me he'd made reservations for a special dinner the next day."

"Did you go?" He would bet his life she hadn't.

"No."

A shadow flickered across her face. Gabriel had hurt her. She hid it quickly. She was a proud woman, but Matias had seen the knot of pain, outrage, and sadness that for a moment twisted her mouth and dulled her eyes. He would have to be careful in Adra. If he got his hands on Gabriel, the urge to wring his neck might prove too tempting. Ramona wouldn't mind being a widow, but he couldn't rob her of the satisfaction she would feel when she made her husband sign the annulment.

"Gabriel agreed to the marriage because the alternative was, in his words, 'too messy,'" she said. "I thought that if we couldn't love each other, at least we could try to be a team since we were stuck together. After the fight, I knew we would never be a couple. So I settled for leading separate lives. I made him comfortable."

For some reason, that word made him violently angry. "Why didn't you divorce him?"

She gave him a small sad smile. "The agreement my father signed has a ten-year noncompete option. If I divorce Gabriel before the ten years are up, his family will cancel my shipping contracts. If I attempt to hire a different shipping company, I will owe his cousin a huge amount of money in compensation. It will cripple our family financially."

He had a rotten feeling. "And if Gabriel dies?"

"Funny you ask. If Gabriel dies, I will also be fined. Although this fine will be one-tenth of the amount I'd have to pay if I divorce him. His existence is inconvenient to his family. They want him dead without staining their own hands with blood. They expect me to murder him to cut myself free."

Rage swelled in him. "Your father—"

"As I said, he thought I was too soft. This was his lesson about hard choices."

He wasn't sure who he wanted to strangle more, her father or her husband.

Her eyes were clear, her gaze hard. "I won't do it. I will not allow them to force me to kill another human being. I alone will decide whose life I choose to take."

Gabriel was the dumbest man in the galaxy.

Ramona sighed. "My plan was to wait the contract out. Once we got the seco research, I realized that it was the perfect way to get the family's finances on solid ground. We had to find something to replace relucyte, and the seco presented an ideal opportunity. I threw myself into work."

He knew that feeling.

"I didn't expect any marital loyalty," she continued. "I gave Gabriel plenty of money and all the freedom he could handle. All he had to do, literally, the only thing he had to do, was to be loyal to the family. He was incapable of even that. Do you know how he got our files, Matias? He walked into the cyber center, smiled, and downloaded them. Nobody paid him any attention. We'd labeled him harmless and useless for so long that nobody even questioned his right to be there. He walked right out with all of our research. This is the man I married. And now I am done. I no longer care about his family or the fines. I only want to be free of him."

She would be free of him if it was the last thing Matias did.

Ramona shrugged as if trying to take off a restraining garment. "Your turn."

"I needed a law."

"The sixth-level tech embargo," she guessed. "That was you?"

He nodded. "Seco development required importing Kelly-particle agitators. There was no way around it. It would take eighteen months to build them planet side, eight months to set up the factory, and the rest for assembly. We didn't have the time or the funds to do it, but we could buy them for a fraction of the cost. I pulled some strings to get the proposal for lifting the embargo on the Senate floor, but Drewery and his bloc shut it down."

Surprise slapped her face. "You sold yourself to Drewery for the seco research, and we and the Davenports benefited from it."

He smiled. "It sounds bad when you put it that way."

She dragged her hands across her face. "For the love of the galaxy, Matias, why didn't you ask for help? We could've banded together with the Davenports. We have political connections . . ."

"Would you have helped the renegade?"

"For the seco generators? Yes, I would. I would've twisted my family's arms until their elbows were turned backward."

"Lobbying would've taken time. Drewery was a sure bet."

"Just how did that conversation go? I will push a law through if you marry my daughter?"

"Pretty much. I knew he was dirty, although I had no idea how dirty. That I learned later. My initial plan was to bribe him. We met. He must have seen something he liked, because he offered me Cassida on the spot."

She shook her head, and when she spoke, she sounded bitter. "At least I have an excuse, Matias. My father made me do it. But you, you did it to yourself."

"No, I made a strategic decision. It didn't seem like a bad deal. I would have to marry eventually. Cassida is beautiful, intelligent, and charming."

Ramona threw her hands up. "Cassida betrayed you!"

"I didn't say anything about her loyalty. I discussed things with her prior to the engagement. I explained that the life of a kinsman is filled with danger, that one day I might not come home, and if we had children, it might be up to her to raise them alone. I tried to be clear that I worked long hours, but I promised that I would make time for the two of us and if she was in any kind of trouble, I would do everything in my power to fix it. I told her that if she didn't want to marry me, she did not have to. I would make sure her father wouldn't force her, although five minutes of watching Drewery and his daughter made it painfully obvious that he has never forced her to do anything in her entire life. I asked her what she wanted out of the marriage."

Ramona had an odd look on her face. He wasn't sure how to interpret it.

"Believe it or not, she said she wanted me. She was enthusiastic about being my wife, in the traditional aspect of the term. We got along well."

Ramona groaned. "Well, of course she was enthusiastic . . . never mind. Please continue."

"It seemed like everyone would accomplish their goals. I got a lovely wife and the law I desperately needed, Drewery got a kinsman son-in-law, and Cassida got a husband who would keep her in the lifestyle she'd become accustomed to. It was only after we were married that all of us realized that nobody got what they wanted. Except for the agitators. We did get those."

He shook his head. In retrospect, the whole thing seemed idiotic.

"Drewery proved a massive liability," he continued. "Everything he touched was tainted."

"And Cassida?" Ramona asked.

He looked at the stars above his head, feeling the familiar unpleasant tension flood his muscles. "I'm a disappointment to her."

"How could *you* possibly be a disappointment?" She seemed insulted on his behalf.

"I thought we'd covered expectations before the wedding. Turns out that I wasn't taken seriously. Cassida and her mother viewed me as a fixer-upper. A man who with proper guidance and direction would become everything they wanted."

Her eyebrows came together. "And what did they want?"

"Something completely different."

She waited for him to elaborate.

He took a moment to find the right words. He never discussed it with anyone. He never planned to discuss it, either, and putting the tangled mess of thoughts and emotions into complete sentences took effort. It hurt.

"I didn't understand what the problem was at first, so when Cassida began complaining, I tried to make her happy. She said she wanted to do something worthwhile. I offered her a position with the company, but she refused it. She decided to do charitable work, so I gave her a budget. She spent some of it, but she was growing more and more unhappy. Looking back at it, there were clues, small things that at the time seemed insignificant. She complained that someone else got a seat on some charity's board instead of her. I commiserated."

He realized his voice was rising. He'd bottled the frustration for so long it was breaking through. He forced his voice into an even tone.

"She wanted me to attend a dinner with a provincial senator, but I was too busy. I told her to go by herself. She threw a fit, the first of many. She couldn't go by herself, I had to be there. Why couldn't I understand such a simple thing?"

Ramona shook her head. "She did comprehend the concept of running a family enterprise?"

"Only when it came to her family business." His words dripped with bitterness. His attempts to achieve detachment were clearly failing.

"Politics?"

"Yes. She decided to sleep separately." He paused. It still stung after all this time. He'd thought he was over it. "I gave her space. The longer this went on, the more I felt that there was something I was missing. Finally, she lost her patience and explained it to me."

"Oh, I can't wait," Ramona said.

"Being the wife of a kinsman, even a prosperous one, wasn't prestigious enough. Cassida wanted to be married to a man with 'power.'"

Ramona burst out laughing.

Suddenly he felt lighter, as if her laugh had somehow crystallized the absurdity of that declaration and now it was all he could see.

Matias grinned back. "Her perception of power was shaped by her upbringing. For all of her outward sophistication, Cassida is rather sheltered. Her charity efforts were a way for her to enter the upper echelons of society, but she didn't get the kind of reception her mother enjoyed. The best spots went to the spouses of politicians. To be valued, to be important, she had to offer useful access, and nobody who mattered to her wanted access to me. I had to become *somebody*, a man who could grant favors and pull strings. She wanted to make an entrance and have every head turn toward her."

"Did she ever ask you what you wanted? Did you communicate to her that doing what she demanded would make you miserable?"

"Yes. I'm getting to that. About six months ago Drewery invited us for a family dinner, during which it was explained to me that a junior senator position was about to come open and I was guaranteed to take it. I told them I wasn't interested. Cassida's mother demanded to know when I was going to grow up and start doing what was best for everyone. I told her that if she spoke like that to me again, it would be the last time we would ever meet face to face. And then I walked out. Cassida caught up with me at our house. You know that saying, 'flew into a rage'? Well, that night I got a visual demonstration of what it actually meant. She screamed, she threw things, she cried. I had embarrassed her in front of her parents. I was useless and stupid. And ungrateful for all the strings her father had pulled. She hated every moment she had to stay in the room with me because I was so unbearably dense that she wanted to hit me until I started bleeding."

"She's psychotic." Ramona shook her head. "If she had done it to Gabriel, he would have given her anything she wanted. He isn't built for that kind of relentless pressure. He would have just folded and gone along."

He gave her a look.

"Oh."

They shared a few minutes of silence.

"So what happened?" she asked.

"After she was done screaming, I told her that I'd chosen my path. I had responsibilities and goals. I worked hard at making my family safe and prosperous. I wasn't a child. I didn't need to be led or fixed. I wasn't about to sacrifice the future of my family and my own peace of mind to please her or her family. If she wanted the trappings of power she so badly craved, it was up to her to achieve it on her own. I would support her in that pursuit. She told me that wasn't what she wanted and that I was a horrible human being. I told her to expect divorce papers in the morning."

He felt exhausted just remembering it. That was a night he never cared to repeat.

"And yet, you're still married," Ramona said, her voice resigned.

"She joined me for breakfast the next morning. She was apologetic and contrite. She said she was under a lot of pressure from her parents. She didn't want a divorce. She loved me and wanted to make the marriage work. I agreed to give it six months."

"Why?"

He'd asked himself that same question countless times over the last few months.

Matias let out a deep sigh. "Because she cried, and she was sad."

Ramona stared at him.

"I was her husband. It was my responsibility to take care of her just as it was her responsibility to take care of me. Marriage is compromise. The least I could do was try to find some common ground. We agreed that I would place greater importance on her needs, and in return she would try to understand what made me happy. We reached a state of ceasefire. Things were calm."

And he had settled for that calm. He saw that clearly now.

"Occasionally we had dinner together, sometimes we slept together, I made sure to make time for the invitations she wanted us to attend, and she stopped her unrelenting assault on the way I lived my life. We were cordial. I was . . . busy. Very, very busy. I knew Drewery would become an issue eventually, so I took the necessary steps, but getting the seco generator up and running mattered more at the time. I thought everything was settled until the morning you walked into my office."

Ramona smiled at him. "You are a good man, Matias Baena."

"But a terrible husband," he said, his words half self-deprecation, half confession.

She shook her head. "No. Everything I've learned about the Drewerys so far tells me they're a family that plans long term. Kinsmen command respect, but we don't usually get

Ilona Andrews

involved in politics. Drewery's family has been on the planet for only four generations. He thinks his roots are shallow. He was born and raised here, yet he doesn't understand that it's not how long you have been in the province—it's how you conduct yourself that makes you a Dahlian. He wanted the authenticity of the old Dahlia family, and the only way to get it was to marry his daughter to a kinsman."

"True," he agreed.

"Unmarried kinsmen who are heads of their families are in short supply," she said. "Most of us are engaged by the time we hit our late teens in the name of some family alliance. My grandparents even went to another planet to find a secare for my father to marry. And here you were, twenty-eight, at the head of your family, with a solid financial foundation and very few dirty secrets. You were a prize catch. I'll bet you anything that you were discussed at their dinner table long before Drewery decided to suddenly care about tech-sector imports. You were weighed, measured, dissected, and found worthy, and then you were baited and trapped."

He'd considered this possibility before but dismissed it. "Seems like too much trouble to catch me."

The twin moons had climbed high into the sky, the large disk of Ganimede glowing with green and the smaller, brighter Silver Sister spilling pale light onto the woods.

Ramona leaned forward, her eyes open wide.

All around them star flowers bloomed, glowing with delicate white. Their petals curled outward, opening the large bell-shaped blossoms wider and wider. Across from them the largest flower shook once, and a fountain of glittering golden spores rose into the air, floating on the gentle night breeze.

Another flower released its spores, then another. The woods shone with gold. A single shiny spark landed on Ramona's hair.

"You said it would be too much trouble." Ramona's voice was soft and wistful. "I would go through a lot more trouble to catch you. You have no idea how rare you are, Matias. A man who is competent, smart, considerate, loyal . . . a man who blocks a sonic blast so you can escape and throws his arm to shield you during a crash. What woman wouldn't want you, Matias?"

All this time he'd told himself she was off limits. The chain he'd put himself on just broke. He wanted her more than anything, and he desperately hoped he didn't screw this up.

Matias braced himself and went for it. "Do you?"

She raised her head to look at him, and he saw the answer.

Matias cleared the distance between them in a heartbeat. He wrapped his arms around her, crushing her to him. Her body felt amazing, strong, flexible yet soft, the same way it felt when they danced. The mere touch of her skin overwhelmed him, cutting through logic and reason. Nothing else mattered except her. He buried his right hand in her hair, breathed in her scent, and kissed her.

The connection between them flared, bursting through him like an explosion. His senses shot into overdrive. He felt her melt against him, the warmth of her, the taste of her tongue, the fragrance of her hair . . . it felt like he had waited for her all his life without realizing it, and now that he'd found her, he'd never let go.

She pushed away from him. It was a small, gentle movement, but it cut him like a knife. He looked at her face and saw tears in her eyes.

"I can't," she whispered. "We can't. We're still married."

He didn't care.

"Let go, Matias."

He did. It almost killed him, but he opened his arms and watched her rise and walk away into the shimmering woods.

CHAPTER 9

The city of Adra glittered like a jewel held near a flame. The sky above it turned the deep purple of late evening, the estates surrounding it surrendering to the twilight, but the city itself was bright as day. Countless lamps, simulated torches, and lanterns held the darkness at bay as the happy crowds flowed through its streets, munching on food from the vendors, flying glowing kites, and throwing brightly colored glitter that would melt into nothing by morning.

Ramona moved with the current, acutely aware of Matias beside her. She wore a translucent skirt that shifted colors like an opal, pale at her waist, flashing with green and red as it reflected the light, then darkening to a deep crimson at the hem. Her top, a matching white, left her arms and her midriff bare. Her hair streamed loose over her shoulders, held back from her face by a delicate diadem attached to a diaphanous crimson veil that overlaid her hair. She would have preferred a combat suit, but they needed the element of surprise. The city had assigned the kruga to Kamen Plaza. And the kruga called for veils, gradient skirts, and naked waists.

It was worth it to see Matias in the traditional garb. He wore a white shirt that clung to his chest, formfitting white pants tucked into knee-high crimson boots, and a long vest that resembled a trench coat without sleeves with its hem split into three pieces at midthigh. The light from the lamps played on the carved muscles of his bare arms, and more than one person had given him a long appraising look as they passed. She couldn't blame them. He looked like the hero of some First Wave saga, except that his short hair ruined the illusion. It should have been in a ponytail that reached to his waist. Yes, the hair was definitely a problem, and so was the expression on his face.

"Will you stop scowling?" she murmured. "We're supposed to be having fun."

"I feel like a jackass."

"You look fine. Smile, Matias. You might like it."

He growled under his breath.

An alert sounded in her head. Karion calling. She took it, subvocalizing her words. "Yes?"

"They're here."

A still image unfolded in her mind—Gabriel and Cassida walking across Kamen Plaza, eight guards behind them. Her husband looked dapper in a dark-blue doublet. It set off his blond hair. She allowed herself half a second to scrutinize his face. Golden tan, bright smile, not a trace of worry in his light-blue eyes. Next to him, Cassida radiated tension, her mouth set in a narrow line, but Gabriel was having a lovely time. She could recite what was going through his head, probably word for word. *What a lovely party, look at all the pretty people just like us, soon we're going to get paid, and then we're going to go somewhere new and exciting . . .*

She gritted her teeth.

Another image. Cassida tugging Gabriel closer, exasperation plain on her face.

That's it, dear. That's all there is to him. Don't worry, we're on our way, and it will all be over soon.

They sped up at the same time. Matias must have gotten the same report from his people.

They had briefly considered setting a trap by the plaza and snatching their spouses off the street. But with the bodyguards, the risk of bystander casualties was too high. The Vandals would not give up. They wanted the seco tech, and the only way to stop them was to wipe them out. Letting Gabriel and Cassida join them gathered all their targets in a convenient location they couldn't easily escape.

The street gently curved around a narrow plateau rising from the city like a stone sword. They wove their way through the crowd until they reached the Kamen Gap, a narrow canyon between two plateaus. The crowd thinned. All those without reservations would be barred from entering the plaza, and for a moment they were alone, marching full speed through the passage, round amber lanterns sprouting from the living rock illuminating their way.

All her worries evaporated. The last traces of tension that had settled on her shoulders since she watched the recording of her husband's betrayal left her. It was simple now. Live or die. Succeed and win everything, or fail and lose it all. Either way, it would be decided tonight. She felt light, strong, and ready.

Matias caught her hand and squeezed it. She gripped his fingers, searching for that same connection she'd felt when they danced. It pulsed into her, binding the two of them together, true, honest, without any subterfuge or pretense, and she leaned into the powerful current, eager to test it.

The entrance to the plaza loomed ahead, the two walls on its sides thrusting out like the jaws of some great beast. They walked toward it hand in hand.

A kissing couple lingered on the left, a blonde woman and a man half-hidden by a long pale cloak. As they passed, the man raised his head, and she stared at Karion's face. They kept walking.

"My brother has a girlfriend," she murmured, bewildered.

"Or at least someone willing to kiss him," Matias said.

The enormous stone gates towered before them. The dancing troupe was already here, the couples milling to the right, just outside of the gate, wearing similar clothes. Matias and Ramona joined the dancers. A dark-haired woman nodded to Matias.

A drumbeat started, measured and light, a precursor of things to come. The first pair of dancers joined hands and strode through the gate in time to the beat of the drum.

Flutes joined in, weaving around the drumbeat. One by one, the dancer couples entered the plaza.

The strings caught the melody. The pace quickened.

The last of the dancers walked through the gate. It was their turn. Matias raised his hand. She put her fingers into his. The connection flowed between them, and they glided through into the plaza.

A square of paved stone thirty meters across greeted them. Textured walls rose on both sides, sheer until the top, where ornamental parapets fenced in the spectators seated in small groups at low tables. An older woman in a bright-yellow gown looked directly at them. Nadira, Matias's aunt, sitting at a table with Adra's mayor. Ramona glanced to her right and saw Uncle Sabor smiling at her from the other wall.

Directly ahead, the facade of the hotel emerged from the sheer cliff, its columns and reliefs carved with such care they seemed draped with velvet. Eight people sat on the balcony. Varden, two lieutenants, a large man standing behind them, and to the right, Gabriel and Cassida with two bodyguards.

At the base of the walls, the Vandals sat in small groups, on the traditional padded quilts. They were out of armor, weapons concealed, but their identical haircuts and rigid spines gave them away.

Where was Varden's secare?

The first pair of dancers spun into the plaza, moving in a large circle. The second followed. One by one, the couples caught the rhythm and joined into a choreographed human whirlwind. The pair in front of them took off. Ramona counted to three in her head, and she and Matias twirled into the circle of dancers, taking their place.

Matias's hand under her fingers was rock steady. He caught her waist, and they moved, turning, spinning, breaking apart, and coming together in perfect sync. She counted the Vandals by the walls as she and Matias dashed around the square. Fifty. The party guests were all here.

One circle around the plaza. Two . . .

She breathed in deeply and looked at Matias. Their gazes met. A hot, feral fire danced in his eyes. If he'd had fangs, he would have bared them and howled. Excitement filled her. If they waited too long, she'd burst.

They were about to finish the third circle. The music kicked into high gear. The pair of dancers in front of them slipped to the side, seamlessly escaping toward the entrance.

The group of Vandals was directly in front of them, four men drinking something from tall crystal glasses.

Matias gripped her arm, twisting her sharply, combining his momentum with hers. His fingers opened, and she almost flew at the four soldiers. The seco slashed out of her arms in twin blades. She sliced through the man on her left, and before his head slid from the stump of his neck, she severed the other trooper's skull. Her seco caught him just below the ear. The top of his head flew, flinging blood into the air. Before the remaining two realized what had happened, she stabbed both of them through their necks in a single precise thrust and kept moving.

The other dancers were still spinning, fleeing the plaza pair by pair, and their flowing skirts and flying vests gave her a couple seconds of cover from the other side of the plaza. Nobody on that side saw the kill, and she was moving so fast.

The three Vandals at the next quilt had no time to react. The closest man's eyes widened, and then she was on them, mincing flesh and slicing bones like butter.

Shots popped from the left, and then Matias was there, shielding her with his seco. She painted a bloody line across the third soldier's throat. Matias caught her, and they charged in unison.

The next group jumped to their feet, three Vandals, eyes open wide, pulling sidearms from under their quilts.

It was her turn to shield. She splayed her seco out, while Matias fell on them. They moved back to back. Her force fields swallowed the incoming energy fire, the impact reverberating through her arms. Matias attacked. He ducked, he cut, he thrust. It was over in seconds.

The Vandals at the other wall ceased fire. The remaining soldiers on their side withdrew and formed a silent line blocking the two entrances to the Kamen. The music died.

A slow clap echoed through the plaza. On the balcony Varden stood up. Gabriel stared at her, open mouthed. Cassida's face was bloodless.

During his entire marriage to her, Gabriel had never seen the seco in action. He had witnessed her training, but he'd never experienced the brutality of the actual combat. He never saw the cross section of a human body revealed as the seco cut through flesh. He never smelled the inside of a person suddenly exposed to air. She was sure Cassida had been equally spared. Matias wouldn't have wanted to traumatize his wife.

This was the side neither she nor Matias had shared with their spouses. The killer side, the ruthless side, nurtured and trained since early childhood. The rude awakening must've shocked them.

"Not bad," Varden said.

He wasn't an idiot. He had to have realized that not a single face on the wall seemed surprised, but he didn't seem rattled.

He turned and walked toward the doorway leading from the balcony.

A man shouldered through the Vandal line in front of them. He wore a black combat suit that clung to him, flowing over the contours of his body as if painted on. Muscle corded his tall frame. His skin was spacer pale, his brown hair was cut short, and when she looked into his eyes, she saw the same predatory fire she had seen in the eyes of the original secare unit. It seared her, and for a moment she couldn't focus on anything else.

Varden walked through the line of soldiers and stood next to Lukas.

"You made me wait a week for this?" Lukas nodded at them.

"It's worth it."

"I'll charge you double."

"Get me their arms intact, and I'll pay it."

Her shell-shocked brain finally processed what she was seeing. They looked similar: same spare, hardened build without a trace of softness, same harsh set of the square jaws, same merciless stare, same height . . . twins.

Twins.

The two men split, circling them from opposite directions.

Her instincts kicked in. She turned left, facing Lukas as he stalked across the stones. Matias's back touched hers as he tracked Varden on the right. The brothers moved well, too well. They didn't look upset. Their eyes held no excitement.

"You look soft," Lukas told her.

She didn't say anything.

"Soft and slow," Lukas said.

Fine. She looked at him as if he were a piece of trash she needed to clean up. "You sold your skills to a butcher, just like Leland. Your bloodline is rotten. We'll end your shame today."

He laughed. "Show me."

She sensed Matias's movement, the coiled power in his body shifting. The connection between them seared her, and she moved with him unconsciously, knowing where he would set his feet and which way he would strike.

Two crimson seco rapiers shot out of Lukas's arms. He thrust, almost too fast to see. Her own seco burst from her arms in short straight swords. Ramona leaned out of the way, smashed her right blade onto Lukas's seco, forcing his arms down, and slashed at his throat with her left sword. He dismissed his seco and leaped back. She'd missed him by millimeters.

Varden hammered at Matias with heavy, powerful blows. Matias blocked, knocking Varden's right arm aside, and moved out of the way.

Lukas summoned two slender curved sabers, inviting her to chase him. Instead, she slipped into the space Matias had vacated, her right seco snapping into a rapier, and stabbed at Varden's exposed side.

Varden leaped back, avoiding the blade by a hair.

Matias cut at Lukas and withdrew.

Ramona brushed against Matias, the connection between them surging through her in a hot current. They were still back to back. They had simply switched opponents. The whole thing took a fraction of a breath.

Lukas scrutinized her. He moved left. She turned to follow, and Matias moved with her.

"A pair," Lukas said in a clipped voice.

"You finally noticed," Varden said.

"I've never killed a pair."

"I told you it would be worth it."

Matias attacked.

She felt his intent and threw her seco up in two round shields. Varden pounced on her in a whirlwind of strikes and slashes, shifting the size and shape of his blades on the fly. She blocked him in a controlled frenzy. He hit like a space freighter. Her arms shuddered under the strain. One small mistake, and they were both dead.

Behind her Matias was fighting, fast, precise, and she moved with him blindly, putting all her trust into the connection between them. She felt Lukas attacking and knew Matias's counter. While Lukas lashed and stabbed with calculated viciousness, looking for an opening, Varden hammered at her, trying to overwhelm her with sheer strength and ferocity.

They think I am the weak link.

If Varden could break her down with his blitz, Matias would be caught between the two brothers. They thought she wouldn't last. They were spacers. Neither of the brothers had ever run fifteen kilometers up a mountain carrying a weighted pack and then been told to make his way back if he wanted water.

Welcome to Dahlia. Neither of you will leave here alive.

Matias slashed with his left seco, curving it in midstrike. Lukas smashed his short seco blade onto Matias's sword and thrust with the other seco, forming it into a narrow spike. Matias leaned right, she leaned with him, and the seco missed them by five centimeters, so close she saw its deep, furious red out of the corner of her eye.

A searing agony lashed her shoulder. The scent of blood shot through the air, and for a moment, she didn't know which one of them had taken the wound.

Matias. Lukas's seco had grazed his arm. He was hurt. She couldn't tell how badly. It could be a scratch, or his arm could be hanging by a thread.

Lukas snarled like an animal and launched a flurry of attacks, throwing himself against Matias's injured side. Matias parried. Varden lashed at her, each slice designed to stagger her. The world melted into combat.

Strike, cut, dodge, shield, slash, strike . . .

She had no idea how much time had passed, but all of them were growing tired. Her breathing was labored. Sweat beaded on Varden's forehead. The strain of matching his moves was sapping her strength. This was unlike any fight she'd ever experienced.

He carved at her, aiming for her chest. She formed her seco into two round shields and thrust them in front of her.

Varden's seco flashed, the heavy blades mutating into rapiers. They slid between her shields, curved, and Varden yanked them back, locking his seco with hers and trying to pull her off balance. She dropped her left shield, breaking free, shifted it into a wide blade, and lashed at him. He pounded at it with his other seco, throwing his entire weight into the blow. Her arm dropped. She saw his other blade coming, but there was no time to avoid it. She twisted her arm, trying to block him with her seco.

Not fast enough. Varden's red blade glanced off her seco and sliced her right forearm.

She shied back, Matias moving with her. Hot blood drenched her arm, dripping to the stones. She willed her right seco into a shield, and the red force field obeyed. The arm still moved. He hadn't hit anything vital.

Varden smiled at her.

Rage flooded her, hot and boiling, not her own, but streaming from Matias through their connection.

They had to end this.

Varden leaped. The world slowed, each instant stretching, each line of his body crystal clear. His seco turned into narrow curved blades running the entire length of his forearms like two oversize ax heads. She saw him above them, knew he would come crashing down, but she had nowhere to go. She thrust her shields up, ready for the impact. He would knock her down. There was no doubt about it.

Drop.

It wasn't a voice or a thought. It was an impulse, and it didn't come from her.

The twin seco smashed into her shields, Varden's full weight behind them.

Instead of bracing, she dropped, letting him push her down to her knees. Varden's face loomed above her, colored red by her seco shields. His teeth were bared, his eyes burning with a mad, hungry fire. He looked demonic.

Matias twisted his body. A streak of red shot from him, forming a long slender blade, and bit into Varden's throat. She dropped her seco, pivoted around Matias's legs in a crouch, and thrust her right seco straight up, cleaving Lukas's groin and stomach in a single devastating stab.

Lukas collapsed in a gush of blood and entrails. Behind her Varden's body crumpled to the ground, his hands on his neck in a futile attempt to stem the blood spilling from a second mouth Matias had opened in his throat.

It was over. She was so fucking tired.

The silence was deafening.

A moment passed. Another . . .

The crowd roared.

Matias offered her his hand. She gripped it and rose to her feet.

Matias stepped toward Varden. The fallen secare was still alive, clamping his throat.

"Nicola convoy. Eight years ago."

Varden's eyes bulged.

"Kurt Sommers and his crew are waiting for you on the other side. Tell them I said hello."

He slashed Varden's throat. His head and severed fingers rolled clear.

Fifteen meters away the line of Vandals stared at their beheaded commander.

"Kill!" a voice roared from the balcony.

Ramona jerked her shields up a fraction of a second before the energy fire from the Vandals hit them.

"Ramona?" Matias asked, blocking the barrage next to her. "How bad?"

"I'm fine. You?"

She gritted her teeth against the pain vibrating in her arm. "Never better."

"Good. Let's fucking end this."

They moved in unison, carving into the Vandal line in front of them, shielded from the crossfire by the mass of the soldiers' bodies. They worked their way through, turned, took out the group by the other wall, doubled back, and sliced through the front doors. They cut their way up the stairs and burst onto the balcony.

Varden's two officers and a third soldier to their left, Gabriel and Cassida all the way to the back, on their right.

The huge Vandal soldier hauled a massive cannon to his chest. The plasma launcher fired with a telltale twang. She dashed right, Matias sprinted left. The plasma load landed between them in a brilliant burst of white.

She raced forward, veering in a zigzag. On the right, Matias tore past the group and doubled back. They fell on the three remaining Vandals like blades of shears closing. All three had combat implants. None put up a decent fight, and when she sliced the last of them in half, watching him fall to the ground was almost an afterthought.

~

Matias dismissed his seco and straightened. His shoulder hurt like hell. The seco had only lightly kissed his skin, but it had left behind a ten-centimeter-long gash that burned like fire. A few millimeters to the side and he would have bled to death by now.

Ramona stabbed the first aid syringe into his arm. He saw her coming and let her do it. A cool current flowed through his veins, soothing the pain.

"Ow," he said.

She rolled her eyes. Blood drenched her right forearm and caked the back of her hand. Anger punched him the same way it had during the fight, when he'd first realized they'd hurt her. He would not let anyone hurt her again.

She saw him looking at her arm and shrugged. "It happens."

"Let me see."

She raised her arm. It didn't look good.

"You need a medic."

She made a fist. "It's fine. I pumped it full of coagulant and painkillers. Same thing I gave you. Stop staring at my arm, Matias. We have unfinished business."

What?

Oh.

He pivoted toward his wife. The bodyguard next to her held his firearm by the barrel with two fingers and gently lowered it to the ground. "I'm out."

Matias looked at the remaining guard. "You?"

"Out." The bodyguard took off nearly running, skirting the bloody bodies. His buddy followed.

Cassida stared at him, her face white as a sheet.

"Hello, dear."

Her gaze flickered to the bodies. "You . . . you killed all of them. You're a butcher."

"Yes."

"You can't kill me, Matias. My father—"

"Has left the system by now, I would imagine. In disgrace. Or don't you watch the news?"

"It was you," she whispered. "You ruined everything."

"Yes." He felt a lot of cold satisfaction from uttering that one word.

She stared at him. "How are you still alive? So many people tried to kill you."

Her tone was bewildered, as if she truly couldn't understand why he was standing in front of her. There was no frustration, no anger, just stunned surprise. She was in shock, he realized.

His wife wanted him dead. A week ago, he would have felt something, some splash of bitter emotion, but today it no longer mattered.

"You were supposed to die. Why aren't you dead?"

He nodded at the plaza below painted red with blood. "Because I killed everyone."

Slowly she turned to the plaza, then flinched.

"Look very carefully," he told her.

"I don't want to," she whispered.

"This is what secare are. This is what we do. You and your family never understood that."

She took a step back. Horror twisted her face. Compared to the people she'd gotten in bed with for this deal, he was a saint. But now wasn't the time to explain it to her.

"The files." He held out his hand.

She offered no resistance. "I gave them to Varden."

He stepped to the balcony's rail. Below, his people and Ramona's were moving through the bodies strewn over the plaza. He called to Solei's implant. *"Our data banks are on Varden's body."*

Solei walked out of the crowd and headed for Varden's corpse. From the other side, Karion did the same.

Matias turned back to his wife. A bit of color had come back to Cassida's face.

"That's all you care about, isn't it? Your stupid company. Your demented research. I ran away with another man, and you don't even care."

"On the contrary, I care a great deal."

"You—"

"Quiet," he told her.

She winced and clamped her mouth shut.

Solei emerged from the staircase onto the balcony, carrying a tablet. He brought it over and nodded. "Data recovered."

Karion had performed the same maneuver, offering his own tablet to his sister. Ramona took it. Her face had shut down. Her stare was flat.

Matias wanted to walk over, put his arms around her, and whisper in her ear that they were alive, and everything was going to be fine. Instead, he called up the divorce agreement on his tablet and put it on the table in front of Cassida. "Sign."

She raised her chin. Her hands trembled. "And if I don't? Will you kill me?"

"Do you really want to be married to a butcher who ruined your father?"

She shut her eyes, clenched her fists, and faced him. "I want a settlement. It's in our contract. I'm entitled—"

"No." Fury sparked in him, but he kept it in check.

"Matias . . ."

"You stole from my family. You betrayed me. You'll get nothing."

She recoiled.

"Don't worry," Gabriel said. "Varden's payment should be enough."

Cassida turned to him. "The transfer never went through."

Gabriel frowned. "What do you mean?"

"There is nothing in the account," she told him. "I've been watching it, and there is nothing. There was no transfer."

This was painful.

"There would have been no transfer," Matias said. "They might have honored their word if your father had remained useful, but without him, you have no leverage."

"These men slaughter children for personal enjoyment," Ramona snapped. "They massacre civilians. Why should they pay you when shooting you in the head is so much cheaper and likely more satisfying? Did you not do any basic homework to research the people you were dealing with?"

Cassida opened her mouth, looked at Matias, and swallowed. "What am I supposed to do now?"

"I don't know, and I don't care," he said. "My patience is growing short. Sign it, Cassida. Before I lose my temper."

She grabbed the tablet, signed her name, and sealed it with her thumbprint. The tablet flashed green. The divorce was filed.

Ramona turned to her husband.

Gabriel gave her a soft smile. It took everything Matias had to keep from punching the man in the face.

"I suppose it's time to go home," Gabriel said.

"No."

Ramona's voice cut like a seco blade.

She thrust her tablet at Gabriel.

He took it and studied the screen. His expression turned mournful. "My family won't like this."

"Your family can go fuck themselves." Ramona sounded merciless. "I will send them the recording of your theft, your adultery, and all of this. They are welcome to come down to the planet and talk to me about it."

Gabriel looked at her. "You're so angry."

"Sign," she ground out.

"Let's talk about this," he said. "I don't want to go back. We can make this work."

"It never worked. You never tried."

"We had fun," he said.

"You betrayed me."

"It was a very small thing. I know I shouldn't have left, but she was pretty and persuasive."

"You fucking coward," Cassida snarled.

"It was an interesting adventure. Now I am ready to come home. It's not fun anymore."

Ramona made a choking noise.

Gabriel smiled again, the weak smile of a spoiled child who would take his scolding knowing no real consequences would follow if only he waited it out. "I never meant any harm. I wouldn't have left the planet."

Ramona stared at him. It was a harsh, predatory stare, and it radiated so much menace it penetrated even Gabriel's thick skull.

He took a small, hesitant step back, his expression confused rather than scared. He was obviously not afraid of Ramona. He must've become convinced that no matter what he did, she wouldn't hurt him because he was weaker than her and she'd consider injuring him beneath her. That's how he had gotten away with all of it, Matias realized. He'd simply avoided presenting himself as a threat, and now he was trying to do it again.

"Sign the annulment, Gabriel. You're a chain around my neck, and I'm tired of carrying your deadweight. I would hurry if I were you, before I decide to cut myself free."

Gabriel's expression turned sad and slightly chiding. "I don't want to," he said. "I would be all alone."

That was more than Matias could stand. He grabbed the other man by the throat, dragged him across the table, and held him at his eye level.

Alarm flared in Gabriel's eyes.

Matias opened his mouth and pronounced each word clearly. "I will break you."

Alarm burst into fear. Gabriel turned to Ramona, his eyes wide. She looked back at him, making no move to help.

Matias gripped his throat tighter and squeezed until he saw the precise moment Gabriel realized that no help would be coming. He clawed at Matias's hand. Matias held him for another second and then dumped Gabriel on the ground at Ramona's feet. She held the tablet out. "Sign."

Gabriel signed the annulment and sealed it.

Ramona stared at the tablet as if it was dipped in sewage. Her brother stepped forward, picked it up, slid it into his doublet, and smashed his fist into Gabriel's jaw. Gabriel's eyes rolled back, and he went down like a log. Karion smiled.

"Got it out of your system?" Ramona asked.

"Mostly. I waited years for that." Karion inclined his head slightly to his sister. "I'm only sorry I couldn't do it sooner. I have our aerial ready."

No. Matias stepped forward. His instincts told him that if he let her walk away, he would lose her. "Let me take you home."

Ramona hesitated.

"He's a Baena," Karion said quietly, a warning vibrating in his voice.

Ramona gave him a long look. Matias held his breath.

"I know," she said. "We have some things to discuss. I will see you at home."

Karion sighed and looked at Matias. "She's the head of the family, but she's also my baby sister. You will bring her home before sunrise, or tomorrow I will start a war."

He turned and walked away.

Ramona glanced at Matias. "I'm ready."

They walked together across the balcony toward the stairs. To the left, above a distant mountain range, a star burst like a firework.

Solei's voice echoed through the plaza. "The Vandal cruiser refused to surrender. Rather than confronting our fleet, they detonated their drive. There are no survivors."

The spectators on the walls stood up and cheered.

⌒

Ramona closed her eyes, feeling the slight vibration of the aerial as it sliced through the wind.

After leaving Kamen Plaza, they had stopped at a small hotel booked by Matias's people. She was able to shower and change clothes, and a medic had patched her arm. It was securely sealed now, the searing agony of the seco blade a distant memory.

While she had showered, Karion had sent an image of a big glowing wreck that used to be the Vandal cruiser. It would be up to the diplomats and politicians to sort out the aftermath. She and Matias had done their parts.

Ramona looked out the window. They were flying over the forest, the night sky endless and deep above them.

Matias hadn't said a word since they'd boarded the aerial. A faint scent of balsam from their damp hair spread through the cabin.

"The temple," he said.

She saw the glittering silver threads of the cupola below. Eventually this flight would end, and everything would be over. She would never sit next to him again. She would never hear him call her name or feel his strong arms around her.

"Matias?"

"Yes?"

"I'm no longer married."

He spun the aerial into a hair-raising turn. "Neither am I."

They landed on the terrace. She clicked her harness open, and then he was right there, leaning over her. She touched his cheek, the dark stubble sharp under her fingers, looked into his eyes, and kissed him. She poured all of herself into it—her want, her despair, her overwhelming need to love, even if only once, a man who was worthy of it.

She felt the exact moment he lost it. He crushed her to him, half lifting her out of her seat. His right hand caught her hair, and he kissed her like he would die if he didn't.

She pulled at his clothes. They spun in the cabin, bumping into the seats and the walls, unable to let go of each other. Her back hit the cargo hold door. He pinned her to it, his left hand blindly groping the wall for the sensor. She ran her hands over his jaw, his hair, his arms, wanting more, and almost cried from the need and the desperation. He kissed her neck, nipping at her skin. Electric heat burst through her, all the way into her fingertips. Ramona moaned.

He hoisted her up onto his hips, his hard shaft digging into her flesh in just the right spot. She licked his throat, right over his carotid, the place where a small cut would end one's life. He gripped her tighter, pressing into her. She licked him again, knowing she was the only one on the entire planet he'd allow to touch him there.

The door slid open, and Matias stumbled into the cargo hold and lowered her to the floor. His hands gripped her tunic. He pulled it up, over her head, trapping her wrists with it, and licked her left breast. The sudden heat over her tight nipple sent another jolt through her, and the connection between them exploded, a torrent of sensation that burned through every capillary in her body in an instant. She welcomed it, opening herself to it without reservation, and felt Matias do the same.

They synchronized, and the connection between them roared into life.

Pleasure flooded Ramona. She moaned and arched her back. He pinned her arms, sliding an iron-hard thigh between her legs, and kissed her again, sucking on the tight bud of her nipple, his thumb brushing the other. Her breath came out in ragged, hungry gasps.

An insistent heat began to build between her legs. The power of their bond crackled in her, sending tiny shocks through her body every time they touched.

He caressed her as if he loved her, as if each taste of her was a gift.

She couldn't stand it anymore. She pushed against his hand. He let her go, and she yanked the shirt off her arms and pulled at his clothes. He stripped off his shirt. His body was perfect, hard and strong, each contour of the muscle shaped by fight and practice. His pants followed, and then he was naked and huge and all hers. He dragged her closer, pulled her trousers off, and tossed them aside. For a moment he was above her, on his hands and knees, and his eyes were on fire.

Breath caught in her throat. She stared at him, unable to look away. She loved everything about him. Every line of his harsh body, every scar, everything. The want in his eyes made her giddy. No man had ever looked at her like that. She'd had no idea it was even possible.

"Ramona . . ." His voice was a ragged growl.

She pulled him to her, running her hands over the thick cords of muscle on his back, and whispered into his ear, "Please."

He thrust into her. He felt like heaven, and she gasped.

His hard length filled her, and he thrust again, driving into her in a wild, fast rhythm. She matched him, relishing each thrust. The connection between them vibrated with power, and she melted into it, savoring him in pure bliss.

He shifted his weight, dragged her hips closer, bending her legs, and pushed into her. Nothing else mattered. He made love the way he fought, all in, and she met him halfway in that feverish place where only the two of them existed.

The pressure building inside her crested. She shuddered and climaxed, drowning in ecstasy. His body shook above her, rigid with tension, and he came.

They stayed together, the aerial silent except for the sound of their breathing. Slowly he moved and lowered himself next to her. She curled up beside him, rested her head on his carved biceps, and closed her eyes.

Rain drummed on the roof of the aerial.

It's over.

They had to go back to their lives. Thinking about it hurt. She tried to imagine letting him go and couldn't.

"Marry me," he said.

What?

She raised her head to look at his face. He couldn't have said what she thought he'd said.

"Marry me," he repeated.

She sat up and opened her mouth. All her conflicting feelings tried to come out at once, and she just stared at him, mute.

He sat. His eyes were clear and resolute. "I don't care what my ancestor did three hundred years ago. It wasn't me. I wasn't a part of that. You weren't a part of that. Nobody who was there back then is still alive today. It's ancient history. I'm in love with you. Don't leave me."

She finally managed to make her mouth work. "Are you serious?"

"I have never been more serious, and since it's me, that's saying something."

Yes, yes, yes . . . Ramona stomped on her own brakes. It wasn't just about her. It was about him, his life, his family.

"What if it's not real?" she asked. "What happens when the adrenaline wears off and you regret this?"

"Never." He swore like it was a vow.

If he did end up regretting it, if they disappointed each other, it would hurt so much she wasn't sure she would survive it. "Matias . . ."

He looked desperate, like a man whose life hung by a thread. "I know this more than I know anything. It's never going to get old. It will never wear off. I'm not given to rash decisions. This is real. I know it. I feel it. I know you feel the same. Stay with me. Say yes, Ramona, and I promise you will never regret it."

She had to say no. They had known each other less than a week. *No* was the most prudent answer, the most careful answer, the answer that would keep the peace in both families, that would give them both a chance to redefine their happiness . . .

There would be no happiness for her without Matias.

"Yes," she said. "I'll marry you."

He grinned at her, and she laughed. Suddenly she felt so light and free, as if she'd grown wings. He was everything she wanted, and he loved her. He was hers, this man that made her lose her mind. And she was his.

"You're insane," she told him.

"Probably. Do you care?"

"No."

He kissed her. It was a tender kiss that promised love and care, and she believed it.

They lay back down, and she curled up next to him. "The families will howl bloody murder."

"Do you trust me?" he asked.

"Yes."

"Then the only question is, How much does your favorite uncle love you?"

EPILOGUE

One month later

The two families glared at each other from across the oversize conference table, Baenas on the left and Adlers on the right.

Matias surveyed the gathering, pausing on Ramona sitting directly across from him. She kept her gaze perfectly neutral.

The past month was pure torture. The plan hinged on them staying away from each other. He hadn't known a month could feel longer than a year. If it wasn't for the frenzy of the preparations, he would've gone mad.

At the head of the table Haider Davenport cleared his throat. "Dearly beloved . . ."

Everyone at the table startled.

Damien Davenport gave his husband a long look. "Excuse him. He has an odd sense of humor. As you all know, we are here to discuss the hostile takeover of Adler, Inc., by Baena Corp. I must remind you that you all agreed to meet peacefully on this neutral ground of our offices."

"Also, this table is expensive," Haider added. "Please don't break it."

It was time. Matias leaned forward. "As of today, I own fifty-one percent of Adler, Inc. That gives me the controlling interest over your company."

Karion and Santiago Adler stared at him with open hatred, both a hair away from violence.

"And where did you obtain these shares?" Karion ground out.

"I sold my stake to him," Ramona said. "For one credit."

The entire Adler battle line pivoted toward her. Silence claimed the room.

"Why?" Santiago choked out.

She didn't answer.

"Wait a minute," one of her aunts said. "You own forty-nine percent. Where did the other two percent come from?"

"From me," Sabor Adler said.

The Adlers did another pivot. The Baena side looked terribly smug, including Matias's aunt, who was smiling like a silver shark serpent.

Ramona's favorite uncle shrugged. "He was very convincing."

"Have the two of you lost your mind?" her other uncle demanded. "Now that Baena bastard controls both companies, his and ours."

Ramona cleared her throat. "Actually, that's not strictly true. He only controls one company. I own fifty-one percent of Baena Corp. I bought it from Matias for one credit."

You could have heard a proverbial pin drop.

"Matias!" Nadira said into the ensuing silence. "Why did you sell our company to Ramona Adler?"

"Because it's customary to exchange bridal gifts before the wedding," he said.

Everyone screamed at once.

Matias got to his feet, walked around the table, and offered his hand to Ramona. She put her hand in his and smiled at the two families. The connection between them sparked, as strong as he remembered it. It felt like coming home after a long, terrible trip, and he grinned at her like an idiot.

"The marriage contracts are in your in-boxes," Ramona said. "We signed them and filed them this morning. Have fun coming to terms with it. We have a lunch date."

They headed for the exit.

"He's a renegade!" Santiago snarled.

"Your children will have the Baena name!" Karion screamed.

"Matias Baena!" Nadira's voice cut across the shouts. "Come back here! When is the wedding? You cannot elope! You will shame the—"

The door slid shut, cutting her off midword.

"Once they realize that they are no longer competing for the seco generators, there will be a lot less screaming," Matias said.

"We will have to give them the wedding." Ramona sighed.

"A small price to pay. We will suffer through it, and then we will escape on a long honeymoon."

She looked at him. "To the Provinces?"

"Yes. The agreement with the Davenports has been finalized, and the plan for the merger of the two research teams is in place. We still have three weeks of summer left. I've inherited an amazing summerhouse. It's by the lake, and there is a cherry orchard."

She laughed. "Where to now?"

"To lunch. I found this little place on the Bronze Terrace. They make the best passion cones."

Matias Baena put his arm around the woman he loved. The connection between them zinged, muted for now, but unbreakably strong. They walked to the elevator holding hands.

For the first time in his adult life, he knew that both he and his wife were perfectly happy.

ACKNOWLEDGMENTS

We would like to thank the wonderful team at Montlake for taking our story and making it into a book. We're grateful to Alison Dasho for her editorial guidance and patience; to Cheryl Weisman for the production management, fine tuning, and diligence in making sure everything was done on time; to Susan Stokes for her thorough copyedit; to Sylvia McCluskey for her proofreading; to Kris Beecroft for her art direction; to Lindy Martin at Faceout Studio for her cover design; and to Luisa J. Preißler for the gorgeous cover illustration.

As always, none of this would be possible without Nancy Yost, our agent, and the amazing people at NYLA.

Finally, we'd like to thank beta readers who patiently suffered through the clunky versions of this manuscript and offered their suggestions: Louise McCoy, Katie Heasley,

Francesca Virgili, Loredana Carini, Harriet Chu, and Wendi Adams. Special thanks to Jeaniene Frost—we did "rub some feelings on it"—Jill Smith, and Mod R for the amazing suggestion that drastically improved the final fight.

ABOUT THE AUTHOR

Photo © Lori Balfe

"Ilona Andrews" is the pseudonym for a husband-and-wife writing team. Ilona is a native-born Russian, and Gordon is a former communications sergeant in the US Army. Contrary to popular belief, Gordon was never an intelligence officer with a license to kill, and Ilona was never the mysterious Russian spy who seduced him. They met in college English Composition

101, where Ilona got a better grade. (Gordon is still sore about that.)

Gordon and Ilona currently reside in Texas with their two children and many dogs and cats.

They have coauthored four *New York Times* and *USA Today* bestselling series: the Kate Daniels urban fantasy series, the Edge rustic fantasy books, the Hidden Legacy paranormal romance novels, and the Innkeeper Chronicles, which they post as a free weekly serial. For a complete list of their books, fun extras, and Innkeeper installments, please visit their website at www.ilona-andrews.com.